The
Thomsky
Fluke

and Other Tales

JAY DAVIS

REGENT PRESS　　　　**OAKLAND**

i

Library of Congress Cataloging-in-Publication Data

Davis, Jay, 1970-
    The Thomsky fluke and other tales / Jay Davis.
        p. cm.
ISBN: 1-58790-061-0
    I. Title.

PS3604.A959T47 2004
813'.6--dc22

                                                    2003066815

Manufactured in the U.S.A.
Regent Press
6020–A Adeline Street
Oakland, CA 94608
regentpress@mindspring.com

CONTENTS

PART I

the unlovelies

I SHOOK and cried a pitiful cry. I was overcome by the monstrousness of what had been done. It's true that I ran away at first. I'd leapt to my feet and had run a quarter mile or more from the scene of the accident, but I turned back in the end. Eventually I'd stopped and had caught my breath. I'd collected my wits and had returned to that horrible place. It would be ridiculous to insist that I did not simply disappear from the area as there are several witnesses who can attest to the state I was in, and to my coordinates at the time. I only mention it now to put an end to the rumor that I walked away undaunted. I was by no means calm or in command of my senses but running like a tortured demon, babbling and throwing out my arms in every direction, howling and cavorting like a wild beast!

I'd been preoccupied with my umbrella, with a leaking cup of extraordinarily hot coffee, and with various papers, books and sketches of mine when it happened. It was early in the morning and I was on my way to work,

struggling to protect my head and clothing from the misty
drizzle, attempting to carry too many things at once while
smoking a cigarette, when I heard a loud crunch and felt
the final shivering shudder of a thing on the sidewalk
beneath my shoe ... a slug or snail, I thought. I slipped and
nearly fell, burnt my wrist and cursed aloud. A gust of
wind caused my umbrella to lurch violently sideways.
More coffee spilled on my clothing and I became very
frustrated.

Of course, I could have simply kept on moving. If I'd
continued forward without looking back (which I definitely
did not—although the prosecution will insist quite the
contrary and is in fact basing its entire argument against
me on this single, easily disproved detail) I might have
avoided the entire nightmare. After all, I'd assumed the
thing crushed underfoot had been a bug, not flesh and
blood, but hydraulics and armor; small and insignificant, a
creature without a soul, a programmed micro-machine
with no vision, no meaning: a pest, a robot. The brain of
an insect is but a simple computer, not an organ capable of
reason or of love, of passion or genius, it cannot register
the crudest emotion and a person more sensible than I
might have been glad to have killed it.

The thing, however, had produced a very unbuglike
sort of squeak, you see. Prompted foremost by the unusual
sound, I turned back and beheld a mutilated mess on the
sidewalk behind me. I thought at first what any reasonable
person would think, given the appearance of red blood, the
screeching shriek that it had produced, its yellow-pink
flesh, and the tiny size of the thing. Of course I assumed it
was a baby bird that had been flung out of its nest.

"Poor little bird," I said to myself, shuddering to consider the death sound, the crunching of bones, the pop, and

the slippery squish I'd experienced beneath my weight. I moved in for a closer look, then viewed it, and became irrational, as I've said.

I stumbled off in a stupor. My pulse was weak and rapid, my breathing shallow and strained. I picked up the pace, threw my coffee at a moving vehicle, then ran away beating things with my umbrella, ripping out the pages of my sketchbook and tossing them into the trees. Several people stopped and stared. I was carrying on and probably screaming. At length, my legs began to flail and I fell face first into the city bush. I then realized the magnitude of what had occurred. I had no choice but to go back.

Everything came into sharp and painful focus for me then—umbrellas filing down the alleyway, scars on faces, muddy boots—I expected awful creatures at every turn, suspected every crevice as I made my way back to the scene of the accident. Soaked through to the bone by rain, cold and shivering, covered with leaves and little sticks, I was an object of pity or of scorn to many commuters that morning.

I do not feel obligated to provide further evidence of my intention as it should be perfectly obvious to anyone that I turned back for no other reason than to save the life of the thing, if possible. I certainly did not return to the site with any idea of covering up a crime, and I'd like to remind the ladies and gentlemen of the jury that I could have simply gone about my business as though nothing had happened at all. I specifically deny premeditation of any kind, and reject the guilty verdict in advance.

It is well known that I did not find a snail, or a slug, or some other bug, or a baby bird there smashed on the asphalt. I found a man. Yet he'd been, in his adulthood and fully grown, no larger than the average thumb of a real man. So he was more of a dwarf, really. The abundance of yellow fuzz or fur on his body, the coloration of his head-gear, his roundish physique, and the deep and expressive lines in his forehead indicated to me that this *unlovely* had been in its late forties or early fifties at the moment of death. A crude weapon (a spear that had been fashioned from a sewing needle or perhaps from a safety pin; having at one end of it affixed the severed head of some insect or another) was near the body, along with a little red leather pouch that had probably contained some of his primitive tools, maps of the area, food-scraps, tobacco, and other medicaments. He was clothed in a strap and a blue leather headdress. His beard and fine yellow fur provided him further protection against the elements. His neck was broken. His arms and legs were crushed and contorted so that he resembled a small crab, or large yellow spider. I tore a remaining page from my book, a still-life that had depicted a block of wood and a bottle of wine, and attempted to gather his remains so as to give him a decent burial. I am not a monster. But the gale and the increasing rain inhibited progress. Eventually I gave up and stumbled back to my lonely apartment, leaving him there to the bugs and the rain and the birds and the cats. I lived less than a block away and was, apparently, followed. He was probably the leader.

I meant to turn myself in, mind you, but it seemed that every morning I was running late. I don't usually miss a day of work for no reason and my employer was immediately suspicious. Besides, it seemed I never had the time, lacked a dime or a quarter for the call, and there was also the question of credibility to consider. I'd been institution-alized twice already by then for misdemeanor infractions, had, regrettably, called in more than my fare share of false

alarms, and lived on the poor end of town in a halfway
house by the freeway. Who would have taken the time to
follow through with an investigation? Who would have
taken me seriously or have pretended, even for a moment,
to believe a word of my fantastic report? In short, I neg-
lected to inform the authorities. It didn't take long for the
guilt and horror to overcome me utterly. My dreams were
filled with colorless, disgusting little demons. I would
awake in a cold sweat, turn on all the lights, smoke half a
pack of cigarettes, take twice my prescribed dosage of
medication with a massive bottle of wine, then collapse
on the floor, or slump over my easel, before losing
consciousness. Within a week I could hear them moving
about at night within the walls. I'd discovered evidence of
their operations in and about the perimeter of my
apartment—little campfires made of matchsticks, thread
hanging from the transom—so I captured a cat and held it
hostage in my home.

The fellow had always been very friendly with me, as
I'd once fed him some tuna through the window. He'd
regularly appeared thereafter on the selfsame stoop for a
handout and I sometimes gave him a dish of milk, a piece
of egg, or some cheese to eat. I'm not sure if Adolph, as I
liked to call him, due to his Hitlerian mustache, had had
an owner prior to his brief stay in my apartment, but he'd
come equipped with a rhinestone flea collar bearing the
name and address of a person several streets down, and he
seemed especially well groomed and fed for an outdoor
cat. I kept fresh lettuce, celery, and flour in his dish both
day and night, poured wine or whiskey in his juice bowl
when it had become encrusted, and the two of us became
close friends. Of course, I soon gathered by his behavior
that the beasts had concealed themselves in every corner

of the house. He was constantly sniffing and howling at
the walls, dashing to and fro and exerting himself greatly
to escape. There would be a terrific scuffle in the closet,
then the hissing and romping would continue in the hall,
or under the sink, behind the couch, or in the bathroom
beneath the tub. Yes, he leapt and carried on to such a
degree that I felt my troubles must soon be over. I began
to sleep again at night, found a better job, and had super-
ficial conversations sometimes with imaginary friends.

Adolph often purred and rubbed himself against my
ankles. He was disposed to hurl his body at the door when
I came near it. The cat did not confine these displays to a
base and disgusting request for food or alcohol, and I
appreciated his affection as he, undoubtedly, appreciated
the strides that I had taken to make his life more comfortable in my apartment. I brought him feathers and rubber
bands to play with. I fashioned a wiggling thing from an
electric motor ... this plugged into the wall and terrified the
cat. Adolph most commonly toyed with his blue plastic
egg-half. If I desired some time and space to myself, he
seemed to know right away. He'd slowly stretch and howl
very loudly, yawn or hiss and go curl beneath the tub
again. In fact I sketched him there sleeping many times,
began a series of watercolors with various props placed
about him, and finished an oil painting that suggested an
Egyptian theme and came off quite nicely. I sold this piece
to a neighbor who'd seen it outside drying in the sun.
Adolph was located in the bottom left-hand corner of the
work. He was represented as a hieroglyph.

I bought a bottle of wine with my earnings. I usually
take the quiet streets to Anton's Deli and Liquor. I like to
inspect the fruitberries and other things on my way. I made
a purchase. Then I stopped at the café. The trashcans,

however, were overflowing and it upset me. I thought I
might see a friend or two, perhaps a total of three, walking, talking, smiling, laughing, or merely sitting quietly in
the sun with their muffins, cups, and cigarettes. I'd been in
a fine mood at first, although alone, when, as I've said, I
noticed filth hanging from the receptacle. This laziness
on the part of the coffeehouse management eventually
prompted me to complain. In any case, a line had formed
at the register so that it was by then impossible to reach
the girl in charge. Although it was obviously not my
responsibility to do so, I determined to resolve the problem
myself. I thought I might prove a point and set the example in this way, but things turned out badly. Lifting the
dome-shaped cover at once, I felt something wet on my
fingertips and gave a quick shout. This attracted the attention of a neighboring table. Amidst the giggling gossip, I
was able to remove the lid at length from a cylinder filled
to over-capacity. As trash clattered to the floor and fluid
from a dozen cups or more splattered in every direction,
additional patrons turned their attention to my work. I
became aware of a low murmur in the place. Nevertheless,
I am not the manner of man to stop halfway through a task
under pressure. No! I simply ignored the swine, stuffed all
fallen waste into the clear plastic bag which had by then
been skillfully removed from its container, whilst cursing
them quietly, "Lazy pigs!" I said to myself. Driving home
the last of the trash with my free right hand, I felt something scuttle up the back of my leg and I screamed. It was
a little man. I dropped the bag and my work was undone.
Trash poured forth and all eyes were upon me. When I saw
that dwarves were literally swarming from the sack, I ran
away from the place with my wine, thus narrowly escap-
ing this trick.

The incident set off a series of increasingly unfortunate events, and my nerves began to fray beneath the stress of it all. As I've said, I was relatively happy with my situation for a time. I'd seen my counselor and had found a better job, continued receiving assistance from the state, and had begun to sleep again at night. My luck, however, is bad. On my way out the door one morning, I was stopped in the hall by my landlord. He said there had been a noise complaint. I asked him what it had to do with me, and he accused me of loudness. I said there must have been some mistake, but the man is unreasonable. He is also rude. I find it extraordinarily difficult to control my temper with such individuals. In any case he demanded, as is his way, to know what was then scratching at the door behind me. I listened carefully. I could hear them. When Adolph discovered the creatures there he howled very loudly and hissed them away. The property owner then crossed his arms in front of his body in such a way that I was confined to a small area in the corner. He insisted that tenants to the left and to the right of my unit, specifically, had complained of just such a hullabaloo. I asked him why no one had said anything to me in that case. The man, ignoring my question and crushing in closer, told me there would be a "considerable" rent increase, should I keep the cat. I asked him why. Again he ignored my question and continued, "if and when you move out," or something of the sort. I didn't like the turn which the conversation had taken and told him so, at which point he retorted very rudely that he could evict me at any time as I had, in his view, already broken the lease agreement by keeping an animal on the premises without first informing him of my desire to do so. I raised my voice and rebuffed his remark. He lifted a finger to my face. I screamed, said I would kill him, then dashed out of the building. By then I was already quite late for work.

I began drinking heavily again. I could not afford the dramatic rent increase on my entry-level wage (I'd received a letter several days after the confrontation with Mr. Snively informing me that the terms had in fact doubled) and my cat had been acting foolish. The other borders, having betrayed me to the tyrant, Snively, made no effort to conceal their animosity toward me, and I considered moving away. But where to, and with what money? I found myself in an evil predicament. With two weeks to endure until my next check, my account had somehow come to be overdrawn. When I took this matter up with the clerk, she informed me of an outrageous overdraft fee, and I protested. She apologized, although clearly satisfied to see me suffer, and I brought my fist down heavily on the countertop. I was asked to leave, and did so. With the last of my cash I bought enough wine to get me through the week and went home. The walls were crawling with demons.

Overwhelmed, I stayed at my easel until dawn sometimes. But Adolph could no longer serve as the subject of my studies. The cat had run completely amok. As he could not be stopped from licking his backside obsessively, an ugly bald spot had surfaced near the base of his tail. This unsightly area made a bad impression. It was no longer a pleasure to pet him. His fur was matted and greasy. He'd become sluggish and, seemingly, senile. He stumbled about the room as though drunk, walked into walls, swatted thin air, and frequently collapsed. I thought he was dead many times. In any event he continued to waste away, acknowledging my presence with but a wretched low sound every now and again when I tried to make him eat from the dish. At length, he could only be removed from the litter-box by force. To paint him then was impossible. So I turned again to the still life.

When the alcohol ran out, as indeed I knew that it must, I was unable to sleep. I would lie on my back, although disposed to the fetal position in slumber, and this new direction caused me some anxiety at first. Nevertheless, I feared deformity in reclining thus on one side or the other, as I'd recklessly done throughout my life, and forced myself to lie, as I've said, on my back with eyes directed upward. One night I found myself paralyzed in this position. I could clearly see one corner of the room which included a portion of the ceiling. There had been a small protrusion near the window-top there that was unusual and resembled a baby's hand. Somehow my eyes had fixed on this thing and I could not move them away from it. The thought then occurred to me that I was absolutely vulnerable. I saw something peek from behind one of the plaster deformities that I have described as fingerlike.

"Help! Help!" I said, but no sound came from my throat. It seems to me my lips had been moving, yet silence ensued where a call to nearby humans had been intended. The little man then leapt from the top of the sill and disappeared entirely from my limited field of vision in the direction of my bed. I found I could then move my eyes very slowly toward the foot of the mattress. A tiny shape appeared there. I felt a pinprick in my heel, then lost consciousness.

This happened to me several times. On one occasion, I beheld a sight so horrid and repulsive that I hesitate to recount it here.

An elaborate hallucination? A grisly figment of my

imagination brought on by stress, perhaps? A dream? Yet in dreams one steps into the street and is suddenly naked. In dreams, when walking, for example, one may notice the way is slightly changed. A man is having a conversation with a woman that he never met before, she is overly animated and he loses the flow of what he'd been saying. Then she kisses him on the lips, or leads him by the hand, or pushes him into a car and drives too fast in heavy traffic. Turning to his companion, he finds that she is someone else. The automobile, which somehow was made of cardboard, has now fallen to pieces, and the other cars are blaring their horns in syncopation with his alarm clock. After all, he was asleep and dreaming. The situation was absurd. He wakes up, and when he does, he finds the recent incongruities slowly setting themselves in order again. His teeth have not fallen out. Dogs are not talking. Trees are not walking, nor are the hands of his watch spinning too rapidly, nor melting, neither are they covered with bugs when he looks at the time and finds that it is five to nine. There is brilliant color and a sensible sequence ...

I'd been motionless in bed and awake on my side, for I am absolutely uncomfortable facing upward, when, again, I found my limbs, my eyes, my fingers and mouth paralyzed. Something scuttled to the center of the red woven rug and stood there staring at me with its little iridescent eyes. It made a circular motion in the air with its tiny spear and immediately several more of them appeared in its company. Again I attempted to call out and found my throat unwilling, or unable, rather, to create the desired sound of distress. I could produce no sound at all, fixed in a position on my side enabling me to view their ceremony in its unwholesome entirety. I have said that several of the creatures then appeared in the center of my bedroom on the filthy, tattered carpet. Here they formed a ring of thirty to forty and began to squeal and to dance after one another. They were armed with orange embers, pins, and lengths of string. I thought of Adolph ... then saw him dragged by these things to the ritual circle. They pulled him with wire and stabbed him with their spears. They grimaced and enjoyed themselves so gruesomely, danced and thrust themselves upon his wasted frame so terrifically as the poor beast finally expired, that a fundamental shift in my way of thinking then took place. The determination to act occurred as a matter of course.

The next morning, when I found him there crumpled up, fur brittle with blood, staring into the void, I felt a pressure rising in my chest. Then I held his wasted body for the last time, and of course I cried. But I couldn't stand to touch him then and flung my friend against the window so that it was cracked by the velocity of his dead weight.

He'd been wrapped entirely in their accursed string. I hung him by this bondage from a nail on the front door of my apartment and searched for a shoebox.

I attached his favorite feather, and the blue plastic egg-half that he'd loved so dearly, to this very nail during the search, meaning to bury him properly in a garden of the house adjacent to my shared dwelling, when Snively happened up the stairs, burst into my private premises, and assaulted me physically. I was pulled by my hair to the floor, kicked hard in the ribs, then in the head.

When I came to, I found it very difficult and painful to breathe. I later found large purple bruises over all of my body. My late friend was still there on the door with his most beloved trinkets. I continued that day with the Christian ceremony. He was buried and a prayer was prayed by me, his closest colleague, that did the kitten justice, I believe. Aided thus was he to the peaceful place that none comprehend until they have passed from this existence, alas! fraught full and overflowing with so many nightmares of the flesh.

When I had done this, I proceeded to the hardware store with money from a new check. I bought a large can meant for the containment of gasoline. From thence to the filling station I went, and engaged in another transaction. It is true that I paid cash and headed back to my infested home.

the thomsky fluke

WHILE IMPROVING the user's health and mood dramatically for up to sixteen months, Remeron, a popular substitute for sleep, eventually becomes a problematic necessity. Pharmaceutical company, Strom-Eggers, denies allegations that cumulative side-effects were covered up, maintaining that withdrawal symptoms had not manifested in human subjects at any point during two years of thorough testing. Nevertheless, a massively funded advertising campaign had been organized, and was implemented, in syncopation with research itself. The drug, promising effects of an eight-hour deep sleep on consumers, was released before it was proven safe or even superficially understood.

Strom-Eggers affiliate, WeeCo Inc., has also drawn fire from consumer advocacy groups for presenting Biorganic Citruhistilline, the active ingredient in Remeron, to young adults, and even to small children, with Monkey Dots, a product which could at one time be purchased without a prescription anywhere that its

Quixotic Candies are sold. Marketed as "zany and fun" and as possessing "super-flavors" essential to "going ape wild," each Monkey Dot had up to 40 milligrams of the substance fixed within a brightly colored and extremely tart sugar base. Adult Remeron users, however, had been advised never to exceed the recommended dosage of just 20 milligrams per day.

When it was determined that Biorganic Citruhistilline is highly addictive, all forms of the drug, including Monkey Dots, were pulled from the shelves.

Parents of Remeron Victims (PRV), an Austin, Texas based support group, has been helping children with Thomsky Fluke Syndrome since April, when Chairman Jan Petersen's nine-year-old son, Danny, was diagnosed with the disorder.

"People want to learn more," says Petersen, "because everyone is affected by this."

Sitting in front of the Austin Super Mega Mall, Jan is flanked by her husband, Bill, and by a giant St. Bernard called Sasquatch. The three make an impression on Sunday shoppers. Sasquatch, or "Sassy," entertains a twittering mob of children as Jan and Bill Petersen, in white uniforms with the red letters PRV superimposed on black cotton armbands, distribute literature and collect donations.

"We began to get suspicious when Danny stopped sleeping," Bill Petersen recalls, "so we told him, 'no more candy.' When he started disappearing ... that's when we knew something was very wrong."

Until recently, many used the sleep substitute, Remeron, in order to work longer hours, enjoy more time with family and friends, pursue hobbies, or merely to feel good. Within ten to twenty minutes of ingestion, consumers looked and felt rejuvenated. When taken as recommended, every six to eight hours, seven days a week, crow's feet disappeared, complexions cleared up, and the user began to radiate a healthy "glow." Some appeared years or decades younger within a matter of months. Remeron boosted the immune system, cured arthritis, even sent cancer into remission. Yet, very few people had any idea that Biorganic Citruhistilline is in fact a rare parasite.

Nils Thomsky, a marine biologist working in the Everglades of central Florida, made the first breakthrough discoveries that led to widespread use of the microorganism as an over-the-counter sleep substitute and cure-all drug. Documenting a symbiotic relationship between the efflorescent lampas or "lamp" turtle, and what is now called the Thomsky fluke (a Trematoda class parasite directly related to the extreme longevity of its glowing host) he stumbled on a startling fact.

The lampas turtle never sleeps.

Gorging on flawed RNA molecules until it ruptures, the Thomsky fluke expels its eggs, as well as the amino acid, Citruhistilline, into the bloodstream of its host, a filtration process supplying the ions necessary to rejuvenate worn or damaged cells in the turtle, thus superseding its need for actual sleep. Thomsky believed Citruhistilline might have beneficial effects on humans as well. But he lacked evidence to support this theory, and his discovery did not create much excitement at the time. In a correspondence with Dana Wainwright, Executive Officer of Strom-Eggers Pharmaceutical Co. Inc., he wrote:

"There is no reason to doubt Citruhistilline may be used as a restorative drug in capsule form. Its effect on the (lampas) *turtle is a clear indication of this possibility. You might name such a product 'Remeron,' for instance, as in*

Rapid Eye Movement (REM) sleep ..."

Further research was conducted at the Strom-Eggers facility in Menomonie, Wisconsin, where it was learned that mammals do not provide living conditions suitable to perpetuation of the fluke. If exposed to constant temperatures above 90° Fahrenheit, the microorganism dies within six hours, and humans easily metabolize the unhatched eggs. Any question of a longer living fluke, however, was purely academic. Despite its inability to reproduce in warm-blooded animals, it still released the restorative wonder Citruhistilline. In fact, a short life span made Thomsky's namesake even more appealing to his financiers, as the consumer would always need more to stay awake.

Thomsky had envisioned the manufacturing of a pill containing pure Citruhistilline. As pressure to produce a working time release capsule mounted, however, extraction of the byproduct was abandoned for mass production of the fluke itself.

Nils Thomsky has been missing since January. Journals of his experiments indicate a shocking lack of protocol on the project. The studies conducted in Menomonie were inconclusive at best, yet the product was approved in spite of discouraging or ambivalent results. Two months before his disappearance, Thomsky wrote:

"When Misha was taken off the program, she began to scream, and she has not stopped screaming now for over 36 hours."

Misha, a sympatric gibbon from West Malaysia, disappeared the next day. She had been held on the fifth floor of the Strom-Eggers facility in a large room with no windows and but one heavy, vault-locked door. There was no explanation for the escape, and she has never been found.

If a scheduled dose of Remeron is missed, at any point beyond 16 months of regular use, most will experience severe withdrawal. The first indications are nausea, vomiting, and diarrhea; followed by hot and cold flashes, muscle spasms, cramps, paranoia, visual and auditory hallucinations, and delirium. Violent psychosis, stroke, or heart attack is common beyond six days of abstinence from the drug. Survivors of the brutal comedown sometimes fall into a state of catatonic shock. Others claim to see and speak to creatures from another dimension. Their accounts, although incredibly bizarre, are strikingly similar.

Francesca Lopez, who had been using Remeron to work up to 120 hours per week, had no prior history of mental illness, and is described by work-mates, family, and friends as "down to earth," "levelheaded," and "very reliable." On a two-week trip to Cuba, during which time she'd had no access to the drug, Remeron, she was admitted into the private clinic of Dr. Victor Marcus. She wasted no time in soliciting the staff for Remeron. When Francesca Lopez learned the drug was unavailable in Cuba, she asked for muscle relaxers. Ms. Lopez was informed that only Dr. Marcus, who was at that time with another client, could prescribe narcotics. She then became very emotional, and informed the staff that she had not slept in over eighteen months. Dr. Victor Marcus recalls that she was extremely agitated at the time of her visit:

"Francesca Lopez asked me to close the door on several occasions that morning. Each time she made this unusual request, I showed her that it was already firmly shut, and invited her to observe that it had not been opened at any time since we'd entered the room. She said she was experiencing very serious muscle cramps and asked me to give her something for the soreness in her limbs. I gave Ms. Lopez 250 milligrams of Trazadone, a non-narcotic muscle relaxer, as she seemed genuinely uncomfortable. Then, when she'd calmed down somewhat, I asked her to describe what she was seeing in the room, and she did so. Her response so astonished me that I called my associate, Dr. Evelyn Gardner, to observe the rest of our session. Ms. Lopez then explained to us in greater detail what she perceived in my small office. She said there were eight doors at perpendicular angles to one another, two in every corner of the room. Each of these doors, which were neither evident to my own, nor to Dr. Gardner's perceptions, produced an enormous quantity of light, according to Ms. Lopez, and led gradually downward into vast, dazzling chambers filled with small luminous entities or 'angels,' as she called them. She said that she had not immediately been aware of the doors, but had noticed the corners of the room flickering at a point just before they'd come open. My associate asked Ms. Lopez to trace the border of one of them with her finger, but she refused to do so at first, and told us that the entities were continually moving from one to another of them, and that they looked very unusual. I tried to explain that one of the walls, on which she had described a door, actually separated my office from the street. The client did not believe me. When I opened the window and put a hand into the open air, she screamed.

"When Dr. Gardner and I had calmed the client down somewhat, Ms. Lopez told us that she'd seem my arm disappear into the wall as if I'd been a ghost. Of course, my associate and I had perceived an altogether different series of events. The client, who told us that she had been using the drug, Remeron, for over a year, appeared to be experiencing elaborate hallucinations brought on by lack of sleep. Eventually, she was persuaded to attempt the same experiment on one of her 'imagined' corner portals. If the door, which she alone could see, was real, Dr. Gardner and I had argued, she would be able to walk through it, just as I had been able to put my own arm through the window that we could see but she, evidently, could not. Guided by my associate, the client then stood, took several deep breaths, and slowly approached one of the walls in my office. We did not try to stop her, but instructed Ms. Lopez to move forward very carefully, and to keep both arms stretched out ahead. Of course we'd expected her to stop when she touched the wall. In fact, I had informed Ms. Lopez that she would undoubtedly be halted by the wall in any case. I could certainly not have foreseen the misadventure which followed. Ms. Lopez came within two feet of the barrier and stopped. I asked her why she had done so, and she told me that she was waiting for one of the angels to move out of the way. She seemed very frightened. So much so that I thought it perhaps best to abort the device at that time. Ms. Lopez, however, suddenly rushed ahead. I am unable to account for what followed. The wall separating my second story office from the street is made of solid concrete. I had always considered this structure to be quite sturdy. I had never, and have not since the incident, attempted to walk through the walls of my office. They should be impenetrable to human flesh, yes? Dr. Gardner had already run to the window and I quickly followed suit, but Ms. Lopez was neither to be seen at street level, nor was she hovering somehow supernaturally just beyond the point of departure. She had vanished through the wall like a master magician.

In other words, she'd passed directly through it and had disappeared without a trace. Fortunately, the client was easily called back again, 'Ms. Lopez, that's enough!' I shouted, and she appeared quite suddenly in the corner again. Dr. Gardner had, understandably, found a seat and was unable to speak for some time. I felt there had perhaps been some temporary interference with the clear working of my own mind, and referred Ms. Lopez to a spiritualist."

As disappearances associated with Remeron most commonly occur when scheduled doses are upset or completely discontinued, known users are now processed into centers where they can be closely monitored at all times throughout the lengthy withdrawal period.

At the Sandra J. Hopkins Memorial Clinic in Edmonds, Washington, twenty patients walk in a single file to the cafeteria each morning for breakfast. They follow safety orange lines on the floor which indicate acceptable routes of travel throughout the building. If anyone strays from a line at any time, motion sensitive equipment will trigger a pulsing, high pitched alarm. In the event of such an emergency, patients all stop in their tracks and remain fixed where they stand until a roll call has been taken and everyone is accounted for. Walking with one arm stretched forward to the shoulder of the person ahead, a patient is quickly pulled back by a friend, should they take a wrong turn.

"This is a new regulation," explains Betty Gann, a volunteer at the Hopkins Center, which deals with children and young adults between the ages of eight to eighteen, "We're trying to bring these kids back into a normal life, but it isn't easy. Sometimes they don't even see you. Sometimes they walk right through you."

PART II

THE BELLERO SHIE

HELLO. *Allow me to introduce myself. My name is Richard D. Hoffstettar, Special Envoy to* The Finkle Blasting Company. *If you wish to smoke or stand and stretch, walk around the room ... please feel free to do so at any point during the interview. Later, you will be asked to complete a simple questionnaire. This will be reviewed by a board of judges who, in turn, will forward their results to a committee of executives. They will determine your comprehension of the facts presented to you. Consequently, my own delivery will be reflected in your answers, so please listen carefully.*

no smoking please

SPECIAL TRAINS service the smoking area. Trains run every fifteen minutes and the fare is five dollars round trip. There is no smoking on the train. Heavy security is required at the compound as lines run long and tempers flare. Before entering the area, smokers must log in at the nurses' station and undergo a brief examination. The examination rarely exceeds thirty seconds and traffic is kept flowing at a slow but steady pace. The nurses are friendly people and no one is ever denied the privilege of smoking due to negative test results. In fact, the test is only administered in order to keep statistics completely accurate. Results are forwarded directly to the appropriate agencies via computerized testing machines operated by the nurses.

Smokers must remember to stay on the red line at all times. Having logged in and completed the examination, a smoker will follow the red line into the compound itself. The compound is simply a vast paved area with ten red lines leading to ten red squares. Once inside, traffic tends to move more quickly depending on the city and the time

of day. The red squares are two by two feet in width and
have the numeral *3* and the letters *MIN* boldly stenciled in
black to remind the smoker that, upon entering the square,
he or she has three minutes in which to smoke. In order to
make these three minutes as enjoyable as they should be,
guards with cleverly designed Zippo lighters stand beside
the smoker, usually one guard per square, lighting cigarettes
and making small talk. The guards themselves do not
smoke. Some interesting conversations have undoubtedly
developed only to be cut short by the "thirty second
warning bell." At this point, the smoker has been smoking
and conversing for two minutes and a half and is reminded
to wrap things up. Cigarettes must be snuffed out before
the "three-minute horn" is sounded and the friendly
guards are required to write tickets if they are not.
Continuing on the red line leading away from the square,
the smoker leaves the compound through a heavily guarded
exit gate. Above the gate, stenciled in bold black letters,
are the words *No Smoking Please*.

THE EXECUTIVES *of* The Finkle Blasting Company *employ technology far superior to that available in other markets. The nature of their purpose is obscure and they've skillfully concealed the true identity of all employees from the press. Not even the employees themselves know their own true identities. I myself assume that I am not in fact Richard D. Hoffstettar. I do certainly know that I am in the employ of* The Finkle Blasting Company *as Special Envoy. All orders that I receive, however, are mailed to my residence in Richmond, Virginia without a return address. All I know of* The Finkle Blasting Company *is contained within the following letters:*

the dining room

MOSTLY GLASS and stucco on the outside, sterile white tile and stainless steel within, the restaurants offer a wide variety of fried and grilled food. In malls, amusement parks, airports, and train stations, near tourist attractions, freeway exits, high schools and other hotspots, one may dine or merely observe those who do. Several feet above the heads of the register people, there is a large red digital sign built into the menu board. This reads: meat will be served at (such and such a time). The time could be now. Therefore a line has formed and people are helped by cashiers. They are given soda pop, fried potatoes, and hot apple pie. Most customers request a hamburger bun and receive a tray with an assortment of condiments and vegetables such as lettuce, pickled cucumbers, tomato slices, onions, etc. They pay with cash, credit, or debit card and head for the dining room.

Some people prefer hamburgers on which have been placed a slice of cheese. Those who do line up to the right of a large glass cubicle where curd is pressed into cakes and set aside for curing. The entire process is demonstrated within the cheesebooth. Approximately ten by twenty feet in width with glass panes approaching the ceiling of the dining room stands this popular attraction. Children gather round and enjoy themselves as clear plastic tubes are attached to the udders of a docile black heifer in this area.

There are four employees within the cubicle, two of whom take part in the exhibition, one of which prepares the harness, and another who distributes pre-packed slices through an aperture built into the cheesebooth.

Young persons between the periods of infancy and youth learn that cheese is made of milk that comes from vertebrate animals such as cows.

Some greedy children have already eaten up their slices and they are severely reprimanded by the adults.

The tables are made of plastic and booth seating is also available. A group of related persons, friends, or acquaintances may begin impatiently munching fries and sipping soda. This is acceptable, but meat is not served until the dining room is filled to capacity (at most a ten to twenty minute wait). Children are allowed to re-inspect the cheesebooth or the pulley apparatus that leads away from it, provided they are closely supervised by a parent, older friend, or mature relative.

The dining room becomes a bedlam of delighted voices when the cow is hoisted several inches from the ground, kicking its legs for a moment, unused to weightlessness and the pinch of the straps. When things have settled down somewhat, the cheesebooth door swings open and a complicated system of wheels and cables built into the ceiling begins to move. The cow travels out the door slowly and without effort. It is suspended by two heavy chains attached to the harness. A worker is deployed to keep the children at bay, and walks beside the beast as it glides along, moaning in happy low tones, moving from one end of the dining room to another.

In spite of the rattling chains, the drone of heavy machinery, and the fact that it has reached the larger glass cubicle in the center of the dining room, the creature is calm, content to chew its cud and let its legs dangle. Some children have already taken note of the preparations that are being made within the central showcase, and crowd around the cow as she enters into the open sliding glass door of the beefbooth. Employees form a human barrier so the door may be closed. An atmosphere of tension prevails in the dining room. The uneasiness is sometimes heightened by the cries of the beast, and parents reassure their little ones, either joining them at the glass or ushering them back to the tables. A child somewhere begins to whimper and cheery music is piped in to make dining more pleasurable. The troublesome tot is satiated with pie and the spectacle within the glass enclosure proceeds. Ten employees take part in the exhibition. They work quickly, and pre-cooked patties are pushed through an aperture built into the front of the beefbooth.

IN A *money society, human contact is bought and sold and could some-day become exclusively a matter of money exchange. The subtle forms of prostitution that we are exposed to on a daily basis erode the moral fiber of the human frame, creating an emotional dependence on money and the quick fix of the transaction.*

family food and drug

"AISLE THREE," blared the intercom as Dewey reached his destination, shoe polish. He also needed toothpaste. Rounding the corner and turning left to Health and Hygiene, he stood at the threshold of aisle four.

"Aisle four," came the intercom again.

Dewey, finding it odd that he should be announced at every passage, searched the ceiling with his eyes. Sighting a camera aimed in his direction, he smiled and waved, cheerfully at first, then less so eventually, feeling uneasy and exposed. He took a box of toothpaste from the shelf and headed for the checkout lane.

"Aisle three. Aisle two. Aisle one," the loudspeaker called after him, apparently following his every movement through the store.

At last, he reached a thin cashier and placed his items on the countertop. She passed them over a scanner and his total appeared on her computer along with a digital image snapped of him waving to the camera.

"Three dollars and fifty-eight cents," said the cashier,

attempting to curl the corners of her mouth into a smile.
The effect was quite hideously unnatural.

Dewey searched his pockets. This continued for some
time.

Marking his sheepish look, the cashier then spoke
into a microphone, "Manager assistance, please. Check-
stand one."

"Forgot my wallet."

"No problem," she said, still smiling strenuously, and
handed Dewey a copy of the receipt, "if you wouldn't
mind filling out the void."

He studied the document carefully. Toothpaste and
shoe polish appeared with tax for a total of three dollars
and fifty-eight cents. These items had in fact been voided
out. Date, time, location, register, and employee number
were indicated. A skeletal finger then appeared. It was
attached to the hand of the cashier. This intruding
appendage directed his attention beneath a perforated line
to the heading: *Customer Information*. Here, spaces were
provided for the customer's first and last name, middle initial, date and place of birth, social security number,
address, home and business telephone numbers, etc.

Dewey pulled the slip away from the finger carefully,
but not slowly enough. It squeaked on the countertop.
Turning over the receipt, he noticed a color copy of the
snapshot, along with several questions of a somewhat
more personal nature located above and below it.

"This is a lot of information."

"Not really," the cashier replied quite suddenly, startling Dewey who couldn't be sure he'd really spoken the
words.

"What do you do with this?" he asked, mentally
marking the sound of his own voice.

"Just the void, sir," and she spoke into the microphone again, "Manager assistance. Hurry up, please," then, inexplicably, "Prefer not to what, sir?" She stopped smiling. "Prefer not to what, sir?"

"I would prefer not to fill out this form," he said, backing away.

She grabbed him by the shirt.

"Sir!"

Her claws tightened on his flesh. Then, with a sudden violent shudder, he made for the exit at speed. He found himself on a collision course with several large men. They carried walkie-talkies, wore mirrored sunglasses, white shirts, and running shoes. They would not let him pass. Therefore he turned back again, hoping to clear up any confusion which might have occurred. He was pursued by the men, and by the voice of the intercom which continued to mark his coordinates aloud.

"Aisle three. Aisle two. Aisle one."

Near the register, Dewey met a man with a mustache and a large red tie. Upon closer inspection it could be seen the heavyset gentleman also wore a pin which indicated his name, Brad Neville, and his position, Manager. Dewey felt himself justified in demanding an explanation and proceeded to do so. The manager looked at him and smiled. Dewey raised his voice. Mr. Neville smiled more expansively. Dewey began to shout, then felt a pinch in his neck.

The abducted shopper awoke on a black leather couch in a hot, windowless office.

"Thirsty?" Brad Neville was sitting behind a heavy steel desk on which had been placed a glass of water. "What's your name?"

Dewey rose unsteadily to his feet and consumed the contents of the glass.

"You didn't have identification on you."

"I haven't done anything wrong."

"We just want to know your name."

"Dewey Kenega."

"Dewey? Dewey Kenega? Could you spell that out for me, please?"

Dewey spelled his name for the manager.

"Social security number?"

"I'd like to know what's going on first. Who are you?" he demanded. Then he spit. The water had left a bitter aftertaste in his mouth.

"Mr. Kenega! Please sit down, Mr. Kenega."

"What is this?"

"Water. Care for more?"

"No, thank you," he said, eyeing the glass suspiciously. Already, he felt rather giddy. His stomach tickled. "Who are you?"

"My name is Brad Neville. I am the manager here." The two men stared at one another in silence. "Are you feeling alright, Mr. Kenega? You look a bit peaked."

It was true. Dewey felt very strange. He noticed an ugly mole on Mr. Neville's face and found himself struggling with an inappropriate urge to laugh out loud. The room was small. Smaller still. It seemed to be shrinking. He felt as though his chest and neck were puffing up like a giant balloon. Then his head, his eyes. Suddenly he was blurting out numbers, "Two! nine! five!" he gulped, "eight!"

"I see. That's very good. Please, go on."

"Nine ... ninety-eight! eighty-nine!"

"Two nine five—eight nine—ninety-eight eighty-nine.

That's fine, Mr. Kenega. Now, where do you live?"

More words came from his mouth, but they seemed to originate from a point behind or slightly above and to the right of his head. Had he given the address? "Twenty-two ninety-four Roosevelt." His lips itched. He was leaving his body. It was the most uncanny sensation he'd ever experienced. Although he felt quite helpless, and in spite of the fact that he was horrified, the muscles in his face began to tense until at length he was smiling. The madness of it caused him to shout, "Corner of Main! Apartment three!"

"Right down the street. Twenty-two ninety-four ... apartment three," again, Brad Neville paused and stared at Dewey Kenega. Neither of them spoke. The silence was complete. When Dewey felt himself about to leap out of his flesh, the manager tapped his pencil twice and said, "Let's skip ahead, Mr. Kenega. How did you first hear about Family Food and Drug? Was it a newspaper ad? Television? Word of mouth?"

"The sign!"

"The sign."

"Yes, I'm a regular customer. Living nearby I saw the sign, naturally."

"Naturally. The sign."

"Yes."

"Moving right along, Dewey. What do you like best about Family Food and Drug?" The manager's face seemed huge in the tiny room. Dewey could not look away from it.

"I like the selection and ... it's located very conveniently near my home, as I've said," he began to giggle.

"I see. That's fine, Dewey. Go on and laugh, if you like. Let's see! Would you describe yourself as an outgoing person?"

"No."

"Do you have a lot of friends?"

"No."

"Do you know anyone who does have a lot of friends?"

Again the words poured forth, "Mary Roberts, thirty-one East Deer Street. Edward Matson, eighty-nine-ninety First Avenue, apartment one-twelve. My mother. She has a lot of friends!" he said, becoming hysterical.

"Whew! Let's see ... Edward Matson, eighty-nine-ninety ..."

"First Avenue, apartment one-twelve," Dewey repeated with vigor.

"Eighty-nine-ninety First Avenue. Alright. Apartment number one-twelve, you said? Just try to breathe. Good. We can relax a little. Let me get it all down."

Dewey's face was twisting into a weird red grimace, tears of helpless laughter streamed down his cheeks. And the manager continued.

"Apartment one-twelve. Good," he said, pen scribbling quickly, a bit of sweat forming at the edges of his bushy black mustache, "Where did you say your mother lives?"

EACH DAY, *every person on earth is affected in some way by* The Finkle Blasting Company. *Of course I cannot be completely sure of it, but I possess many letters which seem to indicate that this is the case. I have included a sample that seems to illustrate this rather well.*

several uncanny occurrences

THE FOLLOWING letter is provided courtesy of *The Daily Journal*:

In Memory of Elaine Atkins

I have been a minister for fifty-two years. I've seen many changes in the world, and by the graciousness of God I've lived through many good times. Also, as He saw fit in His wisdom, I have suffered enormously.

My wife, Elaine, passed recently. We shared a blessed and wonderful life together and I will miss her. I don't blame our cat for her untimely death. Rather, I blame the enemy of God who planted an evil seed into that poor, innocent creature.

God rest and keep you, my beloved wife, and please forgive me for what I've done.

REV. CECIL B. ATKINS
First Church of Christ the Sacrifice

POINT OF VIEW
Concerning Occurrences with Cats

An exciting time to be alive? Certainly it is an uncanny time to live on the planet earth. The recent occurrences are totally unprecedented. There is confusion in the streets. The human race is experiencing an epidemic of self-destruction and denial.

A prank millennia in the making. Since Pharaoh's Egypt they've been watching and waiting, sizing up their prey. The most dangerous game! The signal was sent and they quietly unleashed us on ourselves: phase one of a masterful conspiracy. What other explanation can there be? Why, if not in accordance with some nefarious, pre-arranged plan, would literally all of them, in every corner of the globe, begin to behave in this way at once? They knew exactly what course we'd take when they revealed themselves to us, for they know us better than we know ourselves. We should consider this a time of awakening, and of watchfulness, and we should be ready to act, if necessary, with lightning speed.

Some have gone so far as to say the cats will start talking soon. This is a ridiculous hope. They'll keep quiet and continue to reduce the human race as long as we, the hopelessly divided enemy, do nothing to defend ourselves. They advance undeterred, working in unison toward a common goal, while we waste ourselves on drugs and drink. They neither need nor want a meeting of minds with us. In short, they'll go on with the psychological war in silence as long as we allow them to.

The time for action is at hand. We must learn more of their strategies, methods of communication and ultimate goals. It may be necessary to use torture, and, if it becomes evident that we can no longer coexist, we must not hesitate to wipe them out completely. Many will undoubtedly disagree. Many will damn us and insist that we are mad, when in fact it is madness not to act at once.

I was a cat-person once. I, too, sought comfort in the company of these creatures, though I shudder to think of it now. Mine seemed an acceptable companion—quiet, easily placated with food, a dedicated friend possessed of nothing worse than fleas and an enormous bulk of fur. Now the game is up; I see it was a mistake to spare his life. But my initial feeling was of course concern. He seemed extremely ill and I meant to take him to a veterinarian at once. His behavior was unseemly, disquieting. In any case, I turned on the evening news at a point and, with mounting revulsion and horror, realized the scope of the hoax.

Time passed and I became despondent. The sense of betrayal lingered on and I began, like so many, to turn away from the truth.

One day, on my way to the post office, I saw a kitten chasing after a bug near the Hello Café. In my pitiful condition, I was easily taken in by this activity. I watched the little cat, a Korat, pin its prey to the sidewalk. At length the little butcher turned to me with what seemed a vocalization of greeting. He was sitting on all fours like they used to, and I thought he might have been different. Bending low, I slowly approached. Moving closer, I said something senseless in a stupid voice. Then, extending a hand—and grinning, I suppose, much like an ass—I received a painful snub. Oh, how everything's changed! First, moving away quickly sideways, he dodged my foolish advance. Rising evilly on its back paws, like they all do openly nowadays, it then yawned in my face and moved off, gliding away upright on its two hind legs (they

look so strange!) and stopped to whisper with its friends
by the fountain. There were eight or nine of them standing
there. One gave me a dirty look and I lost my head. I ran
over and gave it a kick. And a kick is all it takes to get
them running ... *back on all fours*!

MATHEW RADAR
Staff Writer, The Post

From *The Village Voice*:

It is an exciting time to be alive, just like the front-page
headline says, and I'd like to share a special thing that happened to our family yesterday.

My husband Jack and I were on the back patio with
our two-year-old baby girl. Her name is Julie and she is
always crying very loud. The doctor says it's normal, but
if you could hear her you would know that it's not normal.
Anyway, our tabby-cat named Patches came gliding out
from behind the bushes because Julie was crying as usual.
I think Patches was visiting with his friends again, but it's
hard to tell sometimes because the bushes are overgrown
and there are many shade trees in that part of the yard.
Maybe his friends told him to do it. He stood in front of
Julie, who was throwing a temper tantrum in her stroller,
and then stared into her eyes. He looked very intelligent
standing there like that and when she stopped crying he
reached out his long little arm and put his hand against
Julie's lips. Before gliding back into the bushes he gave
me a look and I could have sworn I heard a voice say,
"That'll keep her quiet, Megan," but it didn't sound like a
cat voice. In fact it didn't sound like a voice at all. It was
more like a thought than a sound, or like hearing a voice
in a dream. It was all so strange, but nothing surprises me

anymore and Julie hasn't cried or eaten too much ever since. Thank you Patches!

MEGAN WILLIAMS
Middleton

THE EXECUTIVES *of* The Finkle Blasting Company *are chosen through a board of directors who, in turn, are selected by a committee of judges who have, by virtue of their excellent service and devotion to the company, earned the right to approve.*

The author of the following is, to the best of my knowledge, in no way associated with The Finkle Blasting Company.

sparky

THE KIDS are grown and Sparky doesn't like to play much anymore. Even when Billy and Sue come home for the holidays, he just sits there by the door, minding his own business. He's a good old dog and a big fella' too. Good old Sparky. We picked him up on our trip out west back in '80. We were camping in Washington state, down by the Nisqually River. Jess had written out a list of supplies we needed, so me and the kids headed for an Indian store I'd noticed down the road a ways. We'd walked about halfway there on the gravel road when suddenly a tiny, gray fur ball jumped out from behind the weeds. He started shaking his tail and jumping into the air, yapping in his happy, little voice. He followed us to the store, licking at our heels and fetching sticks, growling and barking playfully all the way there. There was an old Indian man sitting on the porch of the store. When he saw us coming around the corner, he practically jumped out of his seat.

"Sparky! Come here, you little devil!" he shouted.

The kids looked disappointed when our new friend

took off toward the old man.

"He followed us from the campsite about a half-mile up the road," I explained.

"He's a good little guy," said the Indian, "wild though."

He told us that Sparky's mother was a German Shepherd who'd strayed onto the reservation and mated with his Alaskan wolf dog.

"So that's why he's so feisty," I said.

"I don't know where he gets it," said the Indian, "believe it or not, his dad's a quiet old guy. Maybe it's the Shepherd. We found her and the pups out behind the shed about two months ago. Died giving birth."

At that moment, I wondered if the old man could see the emotion on my face. I turned away toward the kids who were chasing Sparky around the lot. He broke through and jumped up onto my lap. "Good little guy," I thought to myself, "I know how you feel. I know just how you feel."

Well, it turned out that we got to keep old Spark. The Indian had his hands full with his wolf dog and five other puppies. He could tell me and the kids were crazy about Sparky, so he asked us to take him. I wondered if he might have sensed the special connection that I had to the dog. He said Sparky was his favorite of the litter, but he was getting too old to keep up with one like that.

Jess turned out to be a big fan. She always liked cats better though. Maybe that's why she's turned on Sparky after all these years. Just like everyone else has. Everyone but me.

Sparky seemed to love the Midwest, unlike Jess and the kids who were always talking about moving to California. When we got back to Fort Wayne, he made lots of friends in the neighborhood. Winter was his favorite time of year. He loved to play in the snow. He grew up fast and made a good watchdog. In fact, Sparky was a big star there for a while. One night, he surprised a burglar while we were all at the movies. Thief got chewed up so badly he didn't make it out the door and he probably would have died if Jess hadn't called the ambulance first thing when we found him there on the kitchen floor. There was so much blood all over the place I thought he had to be dead already. He wasn't moving and it looked like an artery in his leg was opened up. Jess and the kids were hysterical and I was a little shaky myself. I'd just never seen so much blood before. Sparky just sat there, unusually quiet, watching the body of the intruder, ready to attack again if necessary. The police were asking us a lot of questions as paramedics wheeled the criminal out on a stretcher. Turns out he'd been burglarizing the area for months. They knew it was him because he'd entered the houses with a glass cutter and our kitchen window had been opened the same way. The police kept shaking their heads at the mess, then they'd laugh and pat Sparky on the head, "Good boy, Sparky!"

It turned into a real circus when the newspaper people showed up. They all wanted pictures. Bob White of the eleven o'clock news was there. After taping, he and Jess caught up on old times. Believe it or not, he'd been her date at the high school prom. They were good friends, but had lost contact over the years. I just thought about how lucky I was to have her as my wife. She looked so beautiful standing over there by the news van chatting with her important friends. It made me feel important just to be her husband.

We were a little overwhelmed by it all, but Sparky handled stardom well and never let it go to his head. A lot of neighbors came by with their little tokens of gratitude to Sparky and soon he had a pile of dog bones and rubber toys so big that he didn't know what to do with it all. The kids brought Sparky and all his toys in for show and tell, and enjoyed a new popularity at school.

The next few years were probably the warmest, happiest times of my life. The kids were doing well at school, and I got a promotion at the office, paid off the house, and started setting money aside for Billy and Sue to go to college. We all stuck together and didn't suffer from the problems that other families had. I loved Jess and we just wanted to raise our kids right. They could always come and talk to me about anything. It was a feeling of home and family that I had never known. The void I'd experienced growing up as an only child with just my father to raise me was gone. At the very center of this peace, this easy existence, was Sparky, watching over, keeping it all safe, sharing in the abundance of joy which prevailed at the house.

I'd been introduced to a few of the news people, so Jess and I went out for a drink once with Bob White. I'm not much of a drinker though. I was too drunk to drive after just one cocktail! I had to pass the next time he offered to take us out, but I always insisted that Jess go on ahead without me. I realized the importance of old friends, even though I didn't have any. I guess I've always been a bit of a loner. Boring and shy. I was more of the family type than the socialite. My idea of a good time was going to the park with Sparky and the kids, playing frisbee and cooking wieners. I didn't like all the questions people asked when Jess and I went out with them. When I talked about what I did for a living, they just looked bored. But to me, at that time, my job—my *real* job—was far more important than all the glamour Jess so enjoyed. My job was to build a home for my wife and kids.

Years passed in relative happiness. Then it started. Jess began to pick at me about little things. It didn't bother me at first, but it seemed I couldn't do anything right for her anymore. I was dumbfounded. She'd make me change my clothes three times before I could be seen in public with her. She'd complain if I brushed my teeth with the bathroom door open. Once, she said I was making a whistling noise when I chewed my dinner and that if I wanted to eat at the table I had to chew more slowly. I did everything she asked of me. I only wanted to make her happy again, but nothing worked.

Sparky would listen to me talk for hours. It was silly. He couldn't tell me what to do. He couldn't tell me how to make Jess love me again. Sometimes I wished he was human. I figured he'd have given me some good advice, being such a good listener. He'd just put his big, old head right there on my knee and listen to my problems all night. Good old Spark. Good old dog. The kids were too busy with high school life to pay any attention to me, and I guess they thought I was pretty dull compared to someone like Bob White. The happiness I had enjoyed was slipping away.

It was '92 when the trouble started. I'd been planning a trip to the Grand Canyon since Billy and Sue were almost done with high school. I thought it would be good for us all to go on a big trip as a family again. Nobody seemed very excited at first and Jess told me what a bore I was, but I wouldn't take no for an answer. Anyway, I'd already arranged for two weeks vacation from work. Bob

White showed up at the kid's graduation. No one even cared that I was there. They all flocked around Bob White, the big star. He gave a short impromptu speech, shook Billy's hand and gave Sue a big hug. It all seemed very melodramatic to me. What an actor, I thought to myself, what a bunch of drama!

Later, something strange happened on the way back to the van. Jess had gone on ahead with Bob and when Sparky saw them leaning on his new Corvette, he started barking and growling viciously. Somehow I lost hold of the leash and he took off toward them, then locked his jaws on Bob's left leg! He began to tear at the flesh, and it took me a minute to realize what was happening. Jess was screaming at me to make him stop, but I didn't hear her. Bob just had the funniest look on his face. You get used to seeing these news guys sort of deadpan, expressionless, but he was twisting his mouth and forehead into the most awful grimace I'd ever seen on a human being. At that moment, I imagined all of Fort Wayne tuned into the eleven o'clock news. Bob had that crazy look on his face but he was speaking in a calm voice, reading the meaningless news of the day, making a joke, some clever play on words like he always did. He was explaining to the world that he and my wife had gone to prom together and that they were having an affair. He was explaining what a bore her husband was, and that the man she was married to didn't have a friend in the world except for a dog named Sparky ... a vicious wolf dog which was tearing open his leg and rendering him helpless.

It was a quiet ride out to Arizona. Jess and the kids relaxed in the trailer and Sparky kept me company up front. He was winding down after all his twelve years. Bob White had been good enough to forget the incident at the graduation. Luckily, the police hadn't been involved. Bob would be on crutches for a while though. At eleven he'd be on with his clever jokes and explanations. He'd be thinking of his ratings and his new Corvette. He wouldn't be thinking of us. He'd forget everything eventually.

The campsites were overcrowded so we decided to get away from all the commotion and camp further down river. We headed south and didn't have any problem finding a nice spot somewhere else. Our only worry was that the rangers might give us trouble. We were far enough away from the major tourist area that I wasn't too concerned. It was about a two-hour drive to the nearest gas station. We unpacked our gear and set up there in the dry grass. I felt awkward being alone with Jess and Billy. Sue and Sparky were exploring the trail and I wished I'd gone along. While setting up for dinner, we heard a scream. It came from the direction they'd headed. I was frozen stiff and felt the hairs on my neck stand on end.

"Daddy, help!"

I started running. I didn't know where I was going. Something terrible was happening and I was in a cold sweat, racing over a blur of high grass and yellow rock. I found her there on the trail holding Sparky, trying to comfort him, running her fingers through his beautiful gray fur. Shivering on his side, breathing heavily, his eyes met mine. They were already glassy and distant, but he knew it was me and I think he felt better. I didn't understand what was going on, felt suffocated.

"Dad, it was a snake."

I quit my job today. I'm tired of people who don't even really know me passing judgement or trying to "give me advice," as they say. Even Jess does it. She's more

subtle, but I know what she's up to. When I think of how
things used to be, I just can't believe the way they are now.
I really don't have a friend in the whole world except for
old Spark. Even he gets tired of hearing me talk. He
ignores me most of the time, but I don't blame him. I get
sick of hearing my own voice sometimes. When I'm all
talked out, I just give Sparky a scratch and try to relax.
Doug said he wanted to see me upstairs, but I knew what
he was going to say, so I just put on my coat and walked
right out. I'm tired of being picked at. Pick! Pick! Pick!
Why can't everyone just leave me alone and keep their
mouth shut! There's been so much talk at the office and
around town, so much gossip I can't even walk the dog
around the block anymore. Neighbors staring ... just
because he doesn't get around like he used to. Sometimes
I feel like I'm going insane.

It's sad, but my only solace is being at home alone
with Sparky. He's not so feisty anymore, but we still have
a good old time together. When he puts his head on my
knee and stares up at me like in the good old days, I can
almost forget everything else. I could look into those big,
blue eyes for hours. He'd look right back at me because
we understand each other. We always have. He's getting
too old, I guess, to play rough like years ago, but it's good
for him to get his exercise. We go out back and I throw the
frisbee to him almost every day. He's not so good at catch
anymore. Good old Sparky. Good old dog. It's good for
him to get outside. Sometimes he wants to wrestle a bit,
but I have to be careful. He's fourteen years old now.

I built a higher fence last summer, but I think Sparky
misses the pretty view of the lake we had. He doesn't
understand all the vicious gossip around town. Even if he

did, he wouldn't feel any different about me, just like I don't feel any different about him. I forgot to mention that Billy and Sue have finally made it out to California. I'm glad for them. They come home once or twice a year to see their mother. Nobody bothers with me anymore. They just go in the kitchen and start their silly gossip right away. I hear them in there whispering with Jess. I know what they whisper about. I'm not too far gone to understand what they want me to do. I'm used to everyone acting so strangely but I know Sparky feels hurt and abandoned. I wonder if they even realize that Sparky misses them more than anything else in the world. He sits by the door night and day waiting for them. He waits for the look of recognition that never comes, the approving scratch on the back that no one will give him but me. They just walk on by, too engrossed in their own silly little lives to remember the best friend they ever had. They try to pretend he isn't even there. I don't understand it. Last Christmas Jess and I had finished putting the presents under the tree. It was our family tradition to wait until the kids were asleep on Christmas eve before we brought them out. I noticed Spark there looking lonely by the door so I told Jess to go on up to bed and when she did, I brought him over and opened his present for him. His eyes lit up when he saw the brand new frisbee. It was the kind that whistles when you throw it, but he just saw the new design and all the red rings around it. I guess he liked it so much that he just wanted to look at it for a while, because he was still there in the morning. Nobody said a word. It was so strange. To this day I cannot understand why everyone got so upset. Billy took Sparky back to his lonely spot there by the door and Jess and Sue just cried all morning. Nobody said anything about the presents and I just sat there stumped on the couch until everyone left. Billy came home first. He was drunk. I didn't like him coming home with alcohol on his breath and I told him so. He actually had the nerve to say he was taking Sparky away. Well, when he said that, I felt the blood leave my face and my hands began to shake. I wanted to kill him, my own son. I wanted to give him the beating he'd never had growing up. But I restrained myself and he's never mentioned it again. I wouldn't be so calm the next time.

I don't bother answering the phone anymore. No one ever wants to talk to me.

Jess,

You said you were going to leave me if I didn't get rid of the dog. You said I had one week to say goodbye. Well, that was a week ago today. Goodbye, Jess.

I want you to know that I could never do what you asked. Sparky is the only friend I've ever had that stood by me no matter what. That's more than I can say about you or my very own kids. That's more than I can say about my dad. If my mother was here, maybe she'd understand like Sparky does. I know she would, but there's no point talking to you about anything now.

After the trip to Arizona, I made a will. I want to be preserved, just like Sparky, and I want to be placed next to him there by the door. Please don't try to get out of it. If you do, I promise you'll regret it. That goes for Billy and Sue, for Bob White, or anyone else. I don't mean to sound threatening, and I'm not doing this out of hate. I'm doing it because I cannot bear the thought of leaving Sparky there all alone.

I hope you will remember me the way I was. Maybe you will confess to me, in my harmless condition, all of your adulteries and vanities. When you have done this, maybe you will even find it in your heart to take me over by the tree and sit with me this year. It would be the best present I ever had.

RECENTLY I *met a man who claimed to be employed by* The Finkle Blasting Company *as a Special Envoy. He looked very familiar and I felt certain that I had met him before, although I could not recollect when, where, or under what circumstances such a meeting might have taken place. He gave me a document which bore an authentic company seal, but I suspect that Eric Baumgardner is in fact a fraud of some kind. I have not heard from* The Finkle Blasting Company *in several days, nor have I had any further contact with Mr. Baumgardner.*

the misanthropes

A PERSON living in reverse is like a sponge ... a sponge which is always and miraculously in the right place at the right time. Please consider that we are capable of depositing hundreds, even thousands, of tons of liquid and material waste depending on the duration and dietary habits of our lives. A person will consume an even greater amount than he or she deposits (from a few ounces to several hundreds of pounds more; again depending, among other things, upon the person specifically, the duration of their life, and the eating habits which they have engaged in).

Obviously, the nature, weight, and volume of any deposit is determined by the quantity and character of what has been consumed. The same principle of cause and effect is applicable to a person living in reverse. A man or woman of this kind will experience an extremely difficult and nauseating juxtaposition of normal bodily functions. I shudder to think of it now.

Imagining that anyone would choose to do so deliber-

ately was utterly beyond my comprehension. Yet such a
person I was destined to encounter one day in the supermarket. I witnessed a man taking grapes from his mouth.
He was removing them with his hands and attempting to
conceal them (or so it seemed to me at the time) within the
plastic bag from which they came. I felt quite sickened at
the hideous lack of courtesy which this perverted criminal
had demonstrated and, although I am not usually the type
of person to act on such an impulse, I decided to make a
citizen's arrest. I repeat, I was by the display so entirely
appalled that I felt more or less obligated to do so.

"Hello," I said, "would you care for some assistance?"

He seemed unable to comprehend my simple question
so I took the tone of a grocer whose produce had been
mangled.

"Are you going to pay for those?" I asked.

An odd spasm passed over his face—and he spoke!—
in a tone of voice and in such a grotesque manner (he
slurred and tripped over his words as if some medieval
fiend had possessed him) that I nearly ran screaming from
his presence. My resolve had vanished. I had forgotten my
invisible contract with righteousness, and my sense of
well being was strongly opposed to remaining in such
close proximity to the demon. I felt as if it all must be
some particularly sinister nightmare, and the man was
moaning and hissing in such a way that I should easily
have suspended myself from believing the situation real.
In any case, my feet were fixed to the floor. He was plead-
ing with me, apologizing for the hideousness of his voice,
the strangeness of his dialect, and for his existence in
general. The villain had as of yet, however, made no reference to the food which he had ruined. He was begging
... a simple beggar ... No! I cannot adequately express the

foreign manner of his speech. It seemed horrible ... horrible that he should be speaking, horrible that he should beg in that voice. I felt ashamed for the man and for having interacted with him at all, though I had desired only justice for the working class and for the children of the workers who belonged to that echelon in particular: the factory workers and the future factory workers of our village. I was by then rooted before the devilish buffoon and had been caught up completely in his Mephistophelean ruse. It seemed he meant to take me in and thereby escape the punishment due him, and so he communicated to me—through a series of gestures, gasping vociferations, and unseemly contortions of his face and body—that he was not responsible. That he was living his life in reverse! This did not seem plausible to me. Sensing my uncertainty, he repeated the gestures, convulsive utterances, and odd wriggling. Still unconvinced, I drew his attention to the grapes again. I did not care for his clownish gambols and grimacing (I found my limbs inclined to obey, as they had been loath to do only moments before) and I took the bag in hand, raised it to the face of the garbler, "I accuse you!" my every movement seemed to say. Yet again he expressed profound confusion. Therefore I began a careful inspection of the fruit. Imagine my shock when I found that every grape in the bag corresponded to the bunch by way of an unbroken stem. Not a loose grape in the bag. Each and every grape was attached to its respective branch or shoot and my case was crumbling. I became embarrassed and made preparations to leave the eccentric to his supernatural shenanigans (he was by then chewing and slurping at yellowish pulp which oozed from his chin in abundance) when I bore witness to something which was extremely unnerving. I noticed him kick his foot back as if attempting to conceal something near the base of the produce rack. It was a banana peel. His neck began to move in a way that caused me to feel nauseous. The pulp writhed over his face and the peel leapt into the air. I could not determine if he had caused the thing to jump by some signal force of his will or if the decision to fly had occurred to the object of its own accord. He then captured the inscrutable rind in his hands and occupied himself in a highly distressing series of uncouth and repulsive movements, grunts, and slurping noises. At last, he succeeded in spewing from his mouth, in segments, an entire *unscathed* banana. I watched, enraptured, as he replaced the torn flaps of the yellow fruit, healing the seams as he did so and grafting the stem, with a simple movement of his hand, to some bananas on the fruit rack. Though I had hardly registered the significance of this magic, I felt the mystery of the grapes had been adequately explained.

I experienced no great difficulty in befriending this truly unique individual. After brief introductions, it was discovered that Thomas and I had several mutual acquaintances in common. For instance, we'd had the same landlord once. Although we'd lived in different buildings, and had rented from the man at different times, he became a favorite topic of conversation between us. Soon after our first meeting, which had unfortunately been cut short (we'd both had pressing obligations to attend to at the time), I bumped into Thomas again. I was in line at the same store with a quart of milk and a half dozen eggs. I had not immediately noticed that he was standing in front of me. Only when Thomas began to speak in that unmistakable voice did I recognize my friend. But he wasn't speaking to me. The object of his singular parlance was a woman. I mistakenly guessed that she was his sister. In feature they were quite similar, and in manner identical. Neither of them were particularly unattractive, though both had frightfully pale skin and wild, disheveled hair. The woman noticed my attention and Thomas turned around. I was immediately introduced to Mae Fern (his girlfriend) and given to understand that she, too, existed in a state of polar opposition to the forward flow of time. She began to babble in a language that was unknown to me ... gasping, belching, and sucking down great gulps of air as I had seen Thomas do. Having apprehended my extreme unease (it took me many months to overcome an acute disgust for certain aspects of their manner), Thomas interrupted her ungainly discourse and explained to me that she had commented on the style of my shirt. It seemed to please her. Thomas went on to say that she had been speaking the English language ... in reverse. She had mistaken me for a person who might understand their speech. I shook my head and pointed *forward* so as to clarify my point of view. She smiled and put a thumb over her shoulder: *reverse*. At that point, Thomas stepped up to the cashier and produced a receipt for the can of tomato soup which he had been holding. I detected an unmistakable scowl on the face of the register person. She inspected the proof of purchase and reluctantly opened her cash-box with a key. Then, without so much as glancing in his direction, she pushed several coins across the counter to my friend and took the can between her fingers with evident distaste. The two, who were apparently used to such unaccountable displays of rudeness in the supermarket, politely moved on, making way for me to handle my own transaction. I paid for the milk and eggs and we left the store together. To me, it was raining. To Thomas and to Mae Fern, raindrops were jumping from their puddles back into the sky.

I was intrigued by the couple and began to visit them on a regular basis. On one such occasion, I had found Thomas unwilling to get out of bed. Having already become familiar with several of their unique habits, I attempted to coax him away from his comfortable nest with an empty can. These littered the couple's small apartment and it is no great wonder that the labels they bore, without exception, indicated that they had at some point been, or would at some point be, filled with tomato soup, as sucked (or spit, rather) through a straw, this particular product happened to be their preferred breakfast, lunch, and dinner. It is difficult to describe the many complex and subtle nuances of flavor which occur in tomato soup when it is eaten (for lack of a better term) in reverse. Much of taste perception depends on the specific posturing of taste buds in relation to the food or beverage (object or liquid) being consumed. Therefore, tasted backwards, a banana for instance does not taste like a banana as we know it, but more like a piece of salted fish. An apricot tastes like roast beef, etc.

People living in reverse invariably prefer foods requiring minimal demastication (food which can be spit directly back into the container via rubber hose, flexible plastic tubing, or even a common beverage straw). These people are capable of spitting almost any broth into a bowl or can, but tomato soup is by far their favorite *liquid dinner*.

Just as people living in reverse are incapable of swallowing anything resembling food, we could never retch tomato soup as they do. We belong to completely different worlds.

In any case, I found Thomas that day unresponsive. I insisted that he rise. He grunted. I swore. He roared at me, and I forbore. I then turned to Mae Fern. She was unreading a book of Kierkegaard and had struck half the text from her memory, judging by her upside-down and backward turning of pages to the center of the book.

"Too much sun," she said with difficulty.

"A good downpour. That's what we need around here," came a voice from beneath the covers.

"A thunderstorm!" Mae Fern chimed in.

"But my friends, it's been raining for weeks on end!"

Thomas removed the covers from his body and sat up in bed. He winked at Mae Fern and I was surprised to see a serene (almost happy) expression on his face. He beckoned to me. Then, as I moved closer, he took the empty container from my hand and whispered, "If you say it's been raining, Eric, then I suppose it will."

Pulling back the curtain slightly, he then made a vague observation.

"Dewdrops."

Mae Fern had been glaring at me for several moments and I began to feel as if I'd said or done something to offend her in some way, the more so when she abruptly stood and left the room.

"Yes, the air is very moist," Thomas continued, "I can feel it."

Then, searching for a straw, he began muttering to himself. I couldn't quite make it out, but heard the words "dewdrops," "disgusting," and "horrible," quite clearly and in close proximity to one another. The situation took a sudden turn for the worse when Mae Fern re-entered the room croaking like a bullfrog. Completely at a loss to account for their uncanny behavior, I removed a bag of jellybeans from my coat pocket and thrust several of them into my mouth. (During a severe case of bronchitis I'd bought a pound of these flavorful, bite-sized candies and had found them very helpful in curbing the compulsion to smoke cigarettes. Having recovered completely from my respiratory illness, I discovered that the physical addiction to nicotine had passed—I had not smoked in over three months—but had been replaced by an oral fixation which, though obviously less dangerous, proved to be equally as obsessive. I had acquired an eating disorder which manifested itself in a compulsive and intemperate consumption of gelatin-based candies. Especially in moments of acute discomfort or stress, I was capable of devouring up to a half pound of them at once. I have since reduced my sugar intake by eating only pear or coconut flavored jellybeans. They are more difficult to find. Neither flavor can be purchased at the liquor store near my home.)

"Disgusting! Disgusting!" Thomas repeated.

Having been unable to locate a straw, he was by then retching directly into the can. In despair, I continued to thoughtlessly consume my crutch (my sugary sweets, jellybeans) and had tossed one after another of them into the air, catching them on the end of my tongue. Then I remembered their antipathy for sugar. Almost any concentrated quantity of the substance could be detected by the couple from up to three hundred feet away. Sensory perceptions are altogether unique for those who travel back in time. Lime is not bitter and sugar is not sweet. To these determined few, I've been assured, sugar in particular gives off a repugnant, sulphurous aroma similar to the smell of rotting eggs. Mae Fern was most likely put off by the maliforous scent of candies in my pocket. Gorged orifice agape, stuffed full of the gooey sweets, I realized my mistake. What could have been more horrible to them than jelly beans leaping from the face of a fellow human being?

They did not do things as we do, nor would they have cared to. They were complicated individuals who had at some point perceived a discrepancy with forward time-flow and its relation to life itself. They could not resign themselves to living in the usual way, consuming as great a quantity of liquid and material as possible simply to scribble and excrete, to die and leave the world a rotten, stinking corpse to burn or bury and to consequently be remembered by. No! They were exceptional people determined to reabsorb, regurgitate, and carefully replace anything and everything with which they had ever come into any contact. They meant to painstakingly eradicate all evidence of their existence on earth and return to the womb with total absolution. To them, it is we who are the ludicrous fanatics, adhering as we do to an ideology based on progress. They see us going with the flow into a future where the only certainty is death, and they wonder at our evident lack of direction. Thomas and Mae Fern moved against the tide of time deliberately, acting on a powerful conviction of purpose, but for much too long I was ignorant of this. I sometimes took offense at the evil, lisping manner in which they spoke. I grew sick at the sight and sound of Thomas retching soup. I must admit, moreover, that many of my own pitiful insecurities stood in the way to a deeper, more meaningful understanding of the two.

On occasion Thomas and I would take a stroll somewhere together. He sometimes tripped, more often merely stumbled, due to the fact that he walked backwards. I became irritated eventually, heaped curses on him and hissed that he should be more careful. He didn't seem to hear the rude comments and shouts voluminously bestowed by the local brutes and pitiable urchins. If they had only realized the manner of man he was! In spite of his seeming imbecilities, Thomas was a skilled and persevering genius. He was gifted in so many ways that I began to feel inferior in his presence. He had a perfect memory, for example, which was fortunate because it is always absolutely essential that a person living in reverse be in the right place at the right time, at all times, and according to an almost incomprehensibly strict schedule. If he was to miss one cue, forget even the most trifling detail, the extremely delicate fabric of time itself could be forever torn asunder. He engaged each backward footstep with the balance and intuitive agility of a master tightrope artist. Yet I called him clumsy many times! Had I truly understood the weight of his every word, gesture, and breath ... had I known that each blinking of his eyes *corresponded exactly to the past* ... I would have held my tongue when he stepped on my toes, tripped, or made some seemingly inappropriate sound. He was a man of extraordinary ability, a *genius*, a deft and powerful acrobat, a stickler for punctuality and miniscule detail who lived in total opposition to everyone and everything. And she, too. Mae Fern never ceased to amaze me with her absolute commitment to the life she had chosen.

Needless to say, the couple abhorred sexual relations and frequently expounded upon their distaste, not for children as such (though I was certainly under the impression many times that they were repulsed by the sight or sound of them) but for the production of human beings as we know it. Yet they had a child of their own.

I first became aware of the creature on the eve of our one-year anniversary of friendship. I'd dropped by with several empty cans I'd found in an alley along the way. Mae Fern answered the door. She seemed distressed.

"What have you got there? More cans!"

"I thought you could use the money," I said.

"You shouldn't have come," she retorted.

"Why?" I asked, beginning to feel a bit nervous, the more so when my ears were pierced by a howling shriek. I quickly turned and saw a child by the door.

"Because Seth is back from Grandma's house," said Thomas, who was sitting on the couch, unsewing a button from a black shirt.

Seth was two and a half years old. He possessed a filthy mop of tangled, curly brown hair, and an extremely unpleasant disposition. At first I was quite at a loss to account for another presence there in the room with us. When I realized their relationship to him (and there could be no mistake, he was their son!) I immediately began to reevaluate our relationship. I felt at once that I had been deceived and that I'd even blundered in devoting so much of my time to these backward people. A child! It seemed an awkward, unwholesome element had entered upon the scene; a shameful secret I had rather not had knowledge of. I immediately disliked the monster, and apparently the feeling was mutual. I noticed a stinking, slimy red mess of vomit covering the front of my coat. Seth grabbed hold of my legs at once and proceeded to inhale the dripping ooze before I could take a towel to it myself. He belched and croaked so vigorously, contorted his face and opened his jaws so hideously in order to receive the flying upchuck that I nearly collapsed in shock! I was completely put off by the experience and abruptly bid them goodnight.

My visits became infrequent and eventually ceased altogether. I began to feel ill at ease when their names came up in conversation with one or another of my colleagues, and, in time, it was tacitly understood that any mention of the two was extremely painful to me. Nevertheless, I continued to see them from time to time at the grocery store, more often than not with their child, Seth. As I've said, I saw them only once in a while for a time and during the course of any such awkward collision I could clearly see that the boy was *shrinking*. Imagine my horror when (after almost a year of estrangement) I finally saw them wheeling him through the store in a stroller! I began taking the bus to another part of town to do my shopping, but continued to think of them often.

One dismal Sunday morning in December when I'd found my coffee jar empty, I gathered my gloves and umbrella, buckled up my winter boots, and headed for the café. It was an intolerable day. The wind rushed in every direction. The rain hammered on my vinyl flap. I took the shady streets, ducking under trees for shelter. It was the same route I'd traveled with Thomas many times. That day I mimicked my old friend ... walking backwards against the gale. Then I tripped (on the area in particular that he'd done the same upon so often), cursing at the heavens and sliding sideways through the muck. Thomas had a clever way. He would not have carried on as I did. Nevertheless, I rose to my feet and faced the rain. Then I turned the corner and saw Mae Fern. She seemed to be walking with a limp or possibly she'd put her foot in a puddle. In any case she waddled a bit and looked quite awkward stepping out into the street. Of course ... she was pregnant.

Upon further reflection, and given the perspective a substantial passing of time has provided me, I realize that I simply cannot be reconciled to many of the differences between Thomas, Mae Fern, and myself. I feel there is something inherently wrong with the way they live and I am now inclined to think of my first impression of

Thomas. He had seemed no more than a vandal engaged in a repulsive act of criminal mischief. I doubt there can be any mystery or excitement in life for them. They live each day in tedious repetition of a past they certainly regret, bitterly denounce our normal way of life, recycle soup for cigarettes, and create nothing but chaos.

It is my understanding that Thomas and Mae Fern eventually split up.

FROM: The Finkle Blasting Company
TO: Richard D. Hoffstettar
RE: Finkle Blasting in East Asia

Dear Mr. Hoffstettar:

It has come to the attention of the executives that you have not been checking your mail regularly. Consider this an informal warning, and please be more attentive in the future.

Please release the following information:

1. *Operations in East Asia are proceeding according to schedule at this time.*

2. *Quality control is being maintained.*

3. *New sites are being considered.*

do we need the police?

OFFICER BILL Hock leans against a highly polished Ford Taurus police cruiser. It has been washed and waxed twice today, and is once again parked in front of the Seven-Eleven at the corner of Forty-first and Broadway. He and his partner, Frank Beaver, come here to reminisce.

"Used to be a lot of action around here," says Hock, eyeing cars that move down Broadway at an even 25 m.p.h. "I get sentimental sometimes. Sure, I'd love to write somebody a ticket. It's my job."

Hock is considering alternatives.

"My brother offered to make me a partner in his company in Reno, but this is home. I don't know anything about carpet."

He is consoled by Officer Beaver.

"Think all cops are wishing things would go back to normal," says Beaver, "People have to try and see it from our perspective. To most of us, police work is a tradition passed down from generation to generation. Take me, for example. My father's a cop, my grandfather was a cop, great-grandfather ... You get the picture. There's never been any doubt about it. I was born *cop*." He slaps Hock over the shoulder and continues between bites of a chocolate flavored protein bar, "The way I see it, though, we've still got a job to do: serve and protect. Crime or no crime, there will always be ways of doing that."

We live in a radically different world than that of just twelve months ago. Today, many feel that their tax dollars are being wasted on the maintenance of an antiquated institution: law enforcement.

"Who needs serving and protecting? There's no crime!" Jose Martinez, a local cab driver, feels he has good reason to hold a grudge. The rides or *cruises* that many officers provide his clientele, free of charge, have hurt his business. "It's nice of cops to do this, but they are not thinking of the guys like me with bills to pay and families to feed. Why should anyone pay for a cab nowadays when they can hail a cop ... for free! I can understand that a lot of them are feeling useless. Well, they are. I'm starting to feel the same way, and I'll be looking for a new job, too, unless cops stop trying to be cab drivers. I think they should start a car wash, but right now I'm feeling like—hey! don't do me any more favors!"

Is this the kind of serving and protecting that Officer Frank Beaver has in mind? If so, some, such as Martinez, have had enough.

Back at Forty-first and Broadway, the cars all stop at the stop-line, pedestrians cross in single file, and Officer Beaver has unwrapped another protein bar.

"Bill is taking things pretty much to heart and that's not good," he says, motioning to Hock who is inside having a friendly chat with the proprietor of the convenient store. The two have felt welcome here for years. "I just keep trying to get it through to him that this whole thing has got to be a blessing in disguise. Still, he's right. Hard not to get sentimental sometimes. Used to be plenty of dopers and drunks around here. Not a lot of action for a cop anywhere these days."

There has not been a single criminal conviction anywhere in over a year. In New York City, many officers have already resigned, and the trend is catching on in urban areas across the globe (London, England: fifty-nine resignations; Paris, France: hundreds), but not all officers believe the lawfullness will last. They are hanging on to the hope that crime will make a comeback.

"I don't know why this happened. I won't say I want to see the kind of crime we had, but I can't lie. I wish one of these drivers would run a light. Sure. People aren't perfect. That's why I'm keeping my job! Someone is bound to mess up sooner or later." Beaver has devoured a third protein bar and crumples the wrapper in his fist, seemingly about to toss it to the ground in defiance of the law which he is sworn to uphold. Instead, at the last moment, he winks and places it neatly in the trashcan as his partner emerges from the Seven-Eleven with lunch ... a fresh cup of coffee and a hotdog on a stick.

H: I'm seeing a green meadow covered with yellow flowers ...
C: I was picturing my ex-wife in a chaise longue along the
     Champs Elysées.
H: I see. There's a field nearby?
C: No.
H: Flowers or brilliant colors of some kind?
C: No, not really.
H: I see.*

---

*Hoffstettar, Cavette: *Exercises in Telepathy*, 1966.

spare some change

MINER MIKE has been soliciting donations from the public for nine months and Dorothy Hayes, proprietor of Eats and Treats on Main, is fed up.

"He doesn't contribute anything positive to our quaint little district. Used to be you could come eat breakfast, drink coffee, read the paper, and feel comfortable ... not get harassed every ten seconds! Business is bad, and I feel helpless."

Many are voicing their opposition to the fallen hero, Miner Mike, whose reputation as a loud mouth now has city officials searching for a new alternative.

"I think a lot of people feel left out of the whole process, and that's why the support just isn't there anymore," says Robert H. Doux, Chairman of The One Year Project (OYP) which has been active in community reform since January. "We need to keep enthusiasm high by getting everyone involved in the issue."

Doux believes that ineffectual reeducation techniques, lack of funding, and widespread indifference have crippled the fledgling program and now threaten to derail what he calls "a massive potential for progress."

"Thank-you-thank-you-thank-you ..."

Miner Mike is sitting at the Third Avenue and Broad Street bus stop, downtown. Someone has jammed a stick in his donation pan.

"Thank-you-thank-you-thank-you ..."

He is shrouded from head to toe in lewd graffiti, the handiwork of local hoodlums.

"He looks bad," says irritated commuter, Jane Tipton. "Unless I walk ten blocks to Fourteenth, I've got to catch the bus here everyday, and that's going to mean another long wait with Miner Mike." Tipton says she's been trying to reach an OYP service technician for over a week. "It really gets on your nerves!"

A portion of the recorded message, activated by a triggering device in the 'forty-niner's pan, has been repeating itself without respite since the statue was vandalized a month ago.

"Some of the people I've talked to have been very rude. 'That's not my department,' they say, 'you need to talk to human resources.' So I call human resources and the people there send me right back to the help desk ... 'not my department.' Well, whose department is it?"

Family and friends attempting to locate missing loved ones often become ensnarled in the same bureaucratic loop.

"Obviously, we've still got a few bugs to work out," Doux concedes, "but we're doing all we can to accommodate everyone's needs as quickly and as efficiently as possible. Organization is key. These things just take time and effort."

Some say The One Year Project is taking on too much. Five thousand Miner Mike statues are on the streets today. With an army of sculptors and electricians working around the clock, Doux intends to back up his promise and double the number by November. In less than two months, Miner Mike will beg on almost every street corner in the city. The redwood statues, which depict a rough and tough looking outdoorsman panning for gold, are expected to pay for themselves eventually. Nevertheless, the OYP Chairman maintains that the purpose of the project is not to generate capital, but to "clean up our streets by initiating positive change." And when Robert H. Doux talks about initiating change, he means radical social change ... not nickels and dimes.

I HAVE *not heard from* The Finkle Blasting Company *in six weeks. Distracted, unable to eat or sleep, I've wandered the streets night and day in search of Eric Baumgardner. I know it is unlikely that I will ever see him again or that he is even employed with the company, but I must try to find him. He may have information for me.*

I've just checked the mailbox again. Nothing. Must sleep. I feel myself about to collapse. *

---

*Hoffstettar and I have been close friends for a number of years and have had sensible discussions on a wide variety of subjects. As far as I know, the man is sane and I am deeply troubled by his recent disappearance. On the first Friday of every month, I have visited his apartment in Richmond, Virginia, and have received copies, rewritten in his own hand, of documents sent to him by his employer of ten years, The Finkle Blasting Company (FBC). I have never seen an actual FBC document. In fact, I know little more of the organization than anyone who has ever attended one of Special Envoy Richard D. Hoffstettar's lectures. I print the information he gives me as a personal favor. In no way am I, nor are any acquaintances of mine, other than Hoffstettar, associated with The Finkle Blasting Company.

On Friday, June 4, I was given an apology addressed to the readers of The Bellero Shie. It read as follows:

I DEEPLY *regret that I have no further information to relate at this time. I must admit that I am quite apprehensive at the extended period of time which has elapsed since I have heard from* The Finkle Blasting Company. *Unable to account for the reticent attitude of my employer, I have been attempting to contact Mr. Eric Baumgardner who claims to be working as Special Envoy for* The Finkle Blasting Company. *I have, as of yet, been unable to do so. Again, I would like to apologize for any inconvenience which this has caused the reader of Johnnie Sirani's* The Bellero Shie.

We spoke briefly about The Bellero Shie, Finkle Blasting in East Asia, South Africa, and Afghanistan, and I left him to his papers neatly organized in a pile on his desk. Nothing in his manner indicated mental instability. In fact, Hoffstettar seemed quite calm and collected, as usual. The man eats three square meals a day, abstains from alcohol and tobacco, exercises on a regular basis, and engages in only the most respectable associations. He is invariably groomed to perfection. His clothing is neat and clean at all times. In short, Richard D. Hoffstettar might be called the perfect gentleman. It is not surprising that he was chosen by The Finkle Blasting Company to serve as Special Envoy. He is well mannered, intelligent, and possessed of an excellent speaking voice and stage presence, characteristics that make his public presenta-tion of facts quite interesting and enjoyable. Why the executives would break with Hoffstettar thus abruptly is a mystery to me. In any case, I was completely taken aback when I saw him last at the train station. The perfect gentleman looked as though he hadn't slept in a week. He was unshaven, his clothing was unkempt, and his hair appeared unwashed (it was tangled, greasy, and uncombed). The man was distraught. He nervously wrung his hands together as he spoke to me.

"I've got to find Baumgardner," he muttered, "still nothing. Nothing!"

I was appalled at his appearance, and at his evident state of nervous tension. I suggested a hot bath, but he didn't seem to hear me.

"I'll see you Friday," he said before disappearing aboard a train bound for Miami, Florida.

On the designated day, I went to Hoffstettar's apartment. As I climbed the three flights of stairs leading to his room on the uppermost floor, I became aware of a loud thumping sound coming from above. I approached the door, which I noticed had been left ajar, then pushed open the freely swinging barrier. The place had been ransacked. Overturned desk and dresser drawers lay about the floor, along with loose articles of clothing, silverware, toiletries, and various other of Hoffstettar's belongings. I called out for him. There was no sound but the continued banging of the open front door, the rustle of curtains swelling and lashing out before the windows, and of papers flitting from one end of the room to another caught up in the cross-draft.

For several weeks, I have been attempting to piece together bits of information gathered from his neighbors, friends, and family regarding the last few days before his disappearance. Any information as to Special Envoy Richard D. Hoffstettar's current whereabouts would be greatly appreciated and can be sent directly to the editors of this publication. Thank you.

Johnnie Sirani
The Bellero Shie

PART III

harry higgins

THE UNDEAD smoker, dressed according to ancient Egyptian ritual, did not seem to notice my company there on the porch at first. Nevertheless, I craved nicotine, had the courage and audacity of drink, so could not be deterred from the words, "Pardon me, sir ..."

He flicked a beady eye in my direction and I took this as my cue to continue, "Ah!" but there was no need to go on as he'd at once thrust a hand through the flap in his costume, producing a pack of my favorite brand. I took a cig, acknowledged his generosity with a nod while I lit it, then expressed my thoughts on several topics. As I've said, I was rather drunk at the time and tended to do most of the talking. In fact, the mummy mumbled only three words to me that night. The first occurred toward the end of my monologue on personal hygiene (for the man smelled badly of perspiration and musk) when I came about to asking his last name (a habit of mine—to ask the last name first). He said something like "Mm-gmmm ..." and when I asked if he meant by that, "Higgins," he nodded his head. The second strangled utterance the mummy spoke was

"Mm-mmm ..." which meant "Harold," apparently. The third and last thing he said before rushing off into the darkness was "MMM!" and I took it as a hearty "No!" in answer to my query as to whether or not he might sometimes go by "Harry."

I then returned to the snack tray for a few more crackers, found my party mask and my fiancée, bid several adieus, and escorted Samantha back to her apartment.

Along the way, we talked of many things, including the costumes we'd observed at the Halloween ball, and I asked her if she'd had a chance to talk to the man dressed up like a mummy. She said she had, at great length as a matter of fact, and demanded to know where I'd been during his magic trick which had both startled and amazed the crowd. I mentioned several places throughout the house that I might have been at the time, also making reference to the patio where I'd spent half the night and had met Mr. Higgins myself.

She then slipped her arm from me and sighed, "Sometimes I wish you could be more like Harold."

I took offense and told her so. She moved away. I apologized and wrapped my arm about her waist again. Eventually, we came to the step and I said goodbye. She then slammed the door in my face.

Making my way home, it occurred to me that Higgins had come off as rather a lout, actually. Later in the week, I learned the man had snubbed four male friends of mine at the party, but had been somewhat of a success with the ladies in our group.

I never brought it up again, and Samantha softened at length.

Our wedding took place on the designated day at a cathedral on Sixth Avenue. Monks of The Order of Saint

Gregory inhabited the place. I immediately regretted the choice of venue. The chaste men sang a song that was depressing. Their garb set a somber mood, but we continued. What else could we do?

When we'd given the vows, and the rings, and each other a kiss ... when I'd carried my bride outdoors, and the rice had been thrown, and our mothers had wept ... when the cans on the borrowed car had been dragged through town to the reception, where champagne was duly served, and the excellent food that had been prepared began to be consumed ... I considered the expense, and was further depressed, for I could not help but to feel somehow foolish. I don't know why.

Samantha, however, was in a fine mood, and proposed a toast to the monk at our table that had followed on foot. He was sitting betwixt my sister and a female cousin of the bride. They giggled and poked him with their spoons. Perhaps they were amused at the black hooded robe, the rope, and the graphic rosary he wore. Of course, I found him morbidly out of place at my wedding reception in his veil, and those dirty black leather gloves. In fact, I happened to notice that not an inch of the man's flesh was visible. I frowned. Someone smelled badly. I then blinked. Musk!

"Allow me," I said, "to make the toast," and stood abruptly with my glass in hand. "To Harry, who goes most often by Harold, I think. His last name is Higgins, but I call him just Harry. *Harry Higgins*." And I repeated the words "Harry" and "Higgins" until at length the monk shook a terrible shake (I shall never forget the shake that he shook) and slowly turned his awful veiled face toward me. Indeed it was he. He lunged like an animal. He approached! The women screamed and the men formed a posse when all bore witness to the knife in his insidious grip. Finding himself thus greatly outnumbered, Higgins rushed from the hotel with demon speed.

"My friends," I said, "please allow a new toast ..." and I meant to go on about love and my beautiful wife. Alas! She'd disappeared ... I later learned, in pursuit of her lover.

Only one or two hangers-on remained for the actual meal. I drank myself into an hysterical rage, then ran screaming through the streets until I was arrested.

In jail I learned a detail or two about Mr. Higgins. Most of the prisoners knew firsthand of the lecherous beast. For example, a man who went by the name of "Brass Knuckles" made a typical comment once as we were enjoying the meal.

"Fellow named Higgins ran off with my Sue," he'd said.

Such a statement was sure to set off a ruckus in our section. Many within earshot made loud promises of revenge. Chaos inevitably ensued, and order could be restored but with difficulty in the event of the word "Harold," "Harry," or "Higgins," as all of the men knew of his philandering, and he was passionately hated.

The story was always the same. His modus operandi was obvious: Higgins operated literally under wraps. Any pretext for a covering was sufficient to bring him hither, provided there were ladies available to make the effort of an outing worth his while. I am to this day amazed at the success he had with them. In any event he stank profoundly of musk and other musty stuff, so it must have been the man of mystery image that attracted so many women to him.

Following my confinement I stayed with a friend, for on returning to my room I found the locks had been changed. After two months in jail, I was not surprised to discover new tenants inhabiting the place. My idiot wife had recklessly expended the savings and had overdrawn our account with checks. All of my belongings had therefore been repossessed or were auctioned off to pay the debt. I was in a desperate situation. In my wedding clothes with no money—nor even a wallet with documents to prove my identity—cold, hungry and homeless, I felt fully the weight of the situation that had befallen me. It is not easy to imagine, perhaps, pigeons conspiring to kill a man. Yet the flock's each and every movement in the air or rushing hither and thither in the street suggested some murderous ill will toward me that day. Elderly women do not seem especially dangerous, nay! to those with a crumb in the stomach, for they are not mad with hunger and staring into the hag's face. Sitting at the bus-bench sparing change, I saw their wrinkles deepen, take on malign new vectors, become hateful, cruel, evil. The witches hissed at me like alligators. The waitresses refused me even water, and the young men ignored me when I wanted a smoke, or simply asked them for the time. Everyone seemed to know right away somehow that I was finished, and I wandered the icy streets with nothing and no hope. I was the target of every insult, prey to a limitless hidden dimension of street-life; I was down on my luck and the lunatics knew it. They moved in closer with their yellow talons, whispering curses or shouting aloud, shuffling after me until swallowed—as I knew that I must be also—digested, and metabolized by the unforgiving concrete.

At a point, I was followed by a babbling fiend with blood and filth on his face and clothing. Fearing the worst, though in truth I knew not what the worst might be, I followed paper snowflakes, mistletoe, and bells into a shopping complex for greater safety in the crowd. Slipping artfully from store to store, I soon lost the bleeding bum. Later, I saw him detained by security. This warmed me a bit.

Soon infected by the Christmas spirit, I pretended to shop, eventually convinced myself I'd find a trinket on a shelf somewhere for a dime and a quarter or less, even became obsessed with making such a purchase. Yet the cheapest tinfoil ornament was over a dollar plus tax. Approaching the central mezzanine of the mall, I came to a mini-train carting children through the artificial snow. The North Pole was indicated by a sign on a painted candy-cane post. Here, green elves with bells on pointy shoes capered about Mrs. Claus, a woman of enormous proportion, and led the little ones to a sleigh containing the star of the show, Old Saint Nick. Then I observed that Santa's face was in fact a plastic mask. A chill passed through my body. Not a bit of skin visible! Imagine my indignation when I saw the children kept back from Claus by their mothers, one of whom sat on the covered man's lap laughing like a horse! Whiffing musk, I called his name, for I knew it was he.

"Higgins!"

His head jerked in my direction.

"Harry Higgins!" I bellowed, rushing up the ginger-bread steps to seize him.

He flung his customer with force to the floor—where she sprawled and screamed like an angry goose, legs flying, arms flapping after the scattered contents of her purse—then bolted through the holiday mob with super-natural speed. I gave chase and at length we came to the street. Alas! A parade was in progress and he quickly blended with the crowd. He had escaped.

For many days I wandered aimlessly, taking alms for the poor, and meals from the left-behind plates of light eaters. At night, I slept on commuter trains. Having curled up thus one evening in my cozy seat, I was awakened by a friend.

Peter, who had been the best man at my disastrous wedding, was appalled to find me there thus cruelly reduced to vagrancy. He offered me the warmth and safety of his home, a couch to sleep on until I'd managed a job and some money, and whatever clothes I might need as my tuxedo was by then foul and rancid with the city filth. I accepted his kind offer, of course.

In the evenings we ate celery stew, his staple food (a combination of stalks and vegetable broth that was bland) and things worked out well between us. He was an unstoppable talker, and I was too depressed at the time to cut in very often on the conversations he enjoyed to have with himself in my presence. One night he meaningfully approached the topic of human pregnancy. I offered my own viewpoint, although not very interested in the subject until he mentioned an epidemic of the affliction in our village. He went on to say that many of our mutual friends appeared to be in the process of reproduction. I preferred to avoid any talk of Samantha, but inquired as to whether or not, and, if so, in what condition Peter had seen her since I'd been away. He cleared his throat, put down the soup, raised an eyebrow, and reached for his pipe.

"Well?"

"Pregnant," he said, taking a puff.

"Higgins!" I screamed.

My friend then confessed he'd seen her in a covered man's company many times.

"Pregnant?"

"Unmistakably. Yes. Heavy with child."

"Higgins!" I screamed again, overturning the soup with a flying fist.

Peter gasped. I raked my fingernails over my face. He grunted. I sobbed. He sneezed. I blessed him, and he thanked me. Peter then revealed a painful secret. Olivia, his girlfriend of many years, had run off with Higgins, too, it seemed. They'd met the fiend at an automotive store and service station on MacArthur Boulevard. He (Higgins) had worn the ridiculous costume of a cartoon tire man at the time. A fun-loving girl, Olivia had wrapped her arms around the creature on a sudden impulse. Of course, Peter saw no harm in the gesture at first, and had left them together as he made a purchase. Later, meaning to collect his girlfriend and get going, he found her crazily twirling with the silly man. Becoming annoyed, Peter attempted to cut the fun short. Olivia, however, could only be extricated by threats. On the drive home, she had seemed preoccupied. When he called her the next day, she'd complained of a headache and had cancelled their dinner date. Craving a sandwich in any case, Peter had therefore gone to the restaurant by himself. On the way home, acting on a hunch, he took a detour past the service station on MacArthur again. There, in spite of heavy traffic, and ignoring the jeers of passers by, he found Olivia and the tire man clutching one another disgustingly. Outraged, Peter swerved into the parking lot and honked his horn. Higgins mumbled some nonsense. Olivia, who Peter described as "blushing like a pig," made a scene and told him they were finished. Peter said it was certainly so and returned to his car, heartbroken. He watched Olivia disappear into an alley with her abominable mate, and left the two to their horrid affair.

"Of course I lost all love for her at that moment," he ended.

"But he must be stopped!"

Peter, lighting his pipe, winked and smiled slyly through the smoke.

"Indeed he must, and he will be."

He then reached in his pocket and handed me a small pink enveloped edged with red lace.

"My God!" I said, for it stank of perfume.

"Open it."

I did so. Inside was a silver ticket.

New Year's Eve Ball

Joli Monde *to sing "Je t'aime toujours" and other chansons d'amour*
Interpretive ballet by Les Belles de Toulons
Champagne, hors-d' oeuvres

Admit One

8:00 P. M.
December 31st
Chateau de Danse
16 Vine Ave.

Costume Required

Indeed, it was an ingenious plot. Peter, assisted by Claude Marseille, whose family owned and operated the Chateau de Danse, had planned and prepared everything months in advance. Claude had been done an injustice also, and the fete was in fact a front to attract, capture, and expose the enemy of men: Harry Higgins.

The more I learned, the more I was pleased with their plan, and the more I was glad to have been taken into

Peter's, and at length into Claude Marseille's, confidence.
From the scented admission slips, to the beautiful and
widely famed performers booked—even the venue itself:
a women's school of ballet—all had been brilliantly
conceived and set into motion.

On the anticipated Eve, I was at last introduced to the
smallish, good looking young Frenchman with a nervous
twitch and a bone-crushing grip, Claude Marseille.

"*Ah! Pas du tout! Pas du tout!*" he'd said when I
thanked him for the costume. We three (he, Peter, and I)
were dressed as musketeers for the farce.

There was no time to lose. It was already half past six
when Peter and I had arrived, and several guests were
already milling about the impromptu bar taking drinks.
We therefore removed to the stage behind closed curtains
to rehearse the arrest of Harry Higgins ... much to the con-
sternation of Joli Monde and Les Belles de Toulons who
hadn't yet situated the props for their performance.

"*Sortez!*" said Claude, and we drew our sabers to
chase them away.

"Get out! Out!"

The ladies left without a fight, and Claude placed an
uncorked bottle of excellent champagne between us to
represent the subject of our study. Several scenarios were
then thoroughly worked through. Yet, every time we
seemed to have determined a good point of progress, Peter
was dissatisfied. He'd light his pipe and say, "He'll get
away. Look. Here!" and point in some new direction with
his sword. He had evidently assumed an uncharacteristically
superstitious attitude on the capture of Higgins, who had
become a diabolical figure in his eyes, perhaps inhuman,
maybe immortal.

Here, I inclined to agree with Claude, who laughed,

"*Mais cet homme est stupide.* Only a coward ... no problem, Peter. He is just so ugly. Always in his mask!"

I added that Higgins might suffer from a chemical imbalance of some kind, conceivably due to poor diet, hereditary factors, or simply through overuse of nicotine and alcohol, in which case he would be easily overcome.

We three, uncorking a new bottle, eventually surrendered the stage and mingled with a rush of guests then lined about the food trays for an early snack. The masqueraders were clad, for the most part, in elegant attire with just some secondary mask to meet the advertised admittance criteria. There was, however, a good Pinnochio. In any event, the long nose belonged to no wooden boy, but to a she. The proverbial liar was tellingly big in the belly (as were most of the girls installed about the hors-d'oeuvre table that memorable evening). Olivia, too (who I recognized from a photograph) was evidently in a family way, or "preggies," as Peter put it somewhat sarcastically. She and a girlfriend were dressed as Flappers, and put on airs with a horrid little dog with a smashed in face and a weird brassiere about its waist.

Claude and Peter removed to the vestibule, and I joined them at length.

"Look there!" said Peter at a point.

"It's him!" I said, crushing in.

We beheld a pitiful figure, a man costumed as a ghost, moving with difficulty through the snow. He was covered in a muddy, bloody sheet. This was soiled most notably about the knees.

"He's been attacked already, the bastard!" said Peter.

"*Alors!*" said Claude.

"By dogs," I ventured.

"*Mon Dieu!*"

Higgins continued moving slowly toward us. The wind picked up, and he was nearly disrobed. Then we glimpsed a red pant-leg in shreds.

"He's fallen on hard times," said Peter.

"Attacked by a beast," I insisted.

"*Par des chiens!*"

We could see the ticket in his bulky mitten, then Higgins fell and it fluttered away. He lay motionless in the snow for some time.

Meanwhile, the party was picking up. Joli Monde had been speaking in French as the dancers filed in for the prelude to their exquisite performance, and then there was music, applause, some hooting, and a holler, as I recall. All was going well, and much according to plan, as we set out across the lawn to seize our special guest. The freezing wind slowed us, the gusts of pelting ice and snow drove us from our objective on occasion, but we came upon him through the blinding weather in time to find him still breathing.

"Higgins! Ha!" said Peter, thrusting forth a sharpened sword to stop him should he make a move.

"*Arrêtez!*"

"Take his legs," I said, and we dragged him through the snow to The Chateau de Danse.

What then occurred is completely ridiculous. We stormed the stage with our prey and propped him against a piano.

"Unveil the fiend!" someone somewhere screamed, and the sheet was pulled from his body—but what? ho!—there again the plastic mask of Claus, the red Santa suit, white fur, and black rubber boots.

"Off with the mask!"

The fake bearded face and red suit were removed ...

and then ... a tire man!

"What trick is this?"

"*Diable!*"

Another costume, and another, mask after mask: a monk, a werewolf, a mummy ... a devil, a demon, a man with no head ...

"A Leprechaun!"

"A rabbit!"

"*Un pèlerin!*"

It was nearly midnight and the countdown from ten had begun, but always another disguise, and then other odd stuff: a bottle of perfume with no lid, a dried out dead mouse, a leather-bound book of poems, but still no Higgins.

"Seven! Six! Five!"

A tangle of cheesecloth, a burlap sack, a sock, there was hardly anything more to him ...

"Three! Two! One!"

An after dinner mint, a parking ticket ...

"Hooray!"

Throughout the din, Claude, Peter, and I continued to rip and to grab at the scattered remnants of costumes ... everywhere strewn and thoroughly searched ... until there was nothing left.